AF439702

RED INSIDE

BRIDGETT NELSON

Red Inside

Copyright © 2024 by Bridgett Nelson
All Rights Reserved

ISBN: 979-8-3492-8570-7
Edited by Christine Morgan | Christine-Morgan.org
Cover © 2024 by Wendy Saber Core | SaberCore23Art.com
Book design & formatting by Muzammil F.

This collection is a work of fiction. Names, characters, businesses, places, events, and incidents are either the products of the authors' imaginations or used in a fictitious manner. Any resemblance to actual persons, living or dead, or actual events is purely coincidental.

No part of this publication may be reproduced, stored in a retrieval system, or transmitted in any form or by any means, without the prior permission in writing of the publisher, nor be otherwise circulated in any form of binding or cover than that in which it is published and without a similar condition including this condition being imposed on the subsequent purchaser

For more information about the author, visit
www.bridgettnelson.com

PRAISE FOR BRIDGETT NELSON

"You'll find Red Inside and many more fluids as Bridgett Nelson calls a 'code true' in the ER. It's maniacal creature carnage, and you won't want a cure!"
—Ryan Harding, Splatterpunk Award-winning author of *Transcendental Mutilation* and *Genital Grinder*

"Nelson's debut novella is a bold blend of body horror, creature feature, and survival. The setting and plot are refreshing and unique, and she adeptly takes a popular, but under-utilized, 'monster' and breathes a new life into it on the page. *Red Inside* is wild and creepy-crawly AF."
—Megan Stockton, author of *Lovey, Dark & Deep* and *Bluejay*

"Bridgett Nelson taps into her past experiences as an OR nurse and her love of extreme horror to give us a unique and bloody creature feature with her debut novella *Red Inside*. It's a fast-paced tale filled with gross and gruesome action that will leave the reader cringing and wanting more."
—Eric Butler, author of *The Pope Lick Massacre* and *The Red Stop*

"Can always trust a medical professional to crank up the hospital horror!"
—Christine Morgan, Splatterpunk Award-winning author of *Lakehouse Infernal*

"This book is insane! Grisly, furiously paced, and complete nightmare fuel. I feel unsafe now. Send help."
—Jeff Strand, Bram Stoker Award-winning author of *Demonic*.

DEDICATION

There is only one person I want to dedicate my first novella to…

Jeff Strand
The derp to my duh.
My python baby-daddy.
The wave-maker.
All **the green hearts for you!**

PROLOGUE
DR. FRANCISCO DELGADO

Startled from a dreamless sleep, I awoke to the piercing calls of an Amazonian white bellbird, arguably the loudest bird in existence, trying to find his mate. I sat up, face pressed against the built-in mosquito net of my sleeping bag, heart galloping double-time inside my chest. Pushing the netting aside while licking beads of perspiration from my upper lip, I crawled from the confines of the olive-green polyester surrounding the soft pudginess of my middle-aged body and grabbed my canteen. The water was tepid, but I drank it anyway, frantically gulping the liquid down my parched throat like a lost man wandering the sandy desert.

The tent zipper moved slowly upward. I sat the canteen aside and grabbed my knife, not sure who or what to expect in this godforsaken jungle. A heavily tattooed face peered into my Amazonian domicile, the dark eyes full of worry. Araweeta was the only tribe member who knew rudimentary English. The rest spoke in Yine, an ancient language used by the indigenous people of Peru. Araweeta was Chief Raoni's only son.

Chief Raoni was a first-class prick. I'd heard him arguing with Araweeta about me on two separate occasions. Arguments that always ended with Araweeta saying in English, "He be fine. He be fine."

Was he trying to convince himself?

"Oh, docta. Your eyes open. Goot. Goot." He motioned for me to come outside. I obliged, putting my knife aside and dragging my already dehydrated body into the oppressive heat and humidity of the rich tropical lands along the Madre de Dios River.

Araweeta wore nothing aside from elaborate jewelry pieces around his neck, wrists, and ankles, all of it made from animal bones and teeth. Black tattoos lined his glistening sienna skin. I tried not to stare at the abnormally large sexual organ dangling between his thighs, but how could I not? It was the size of a horse cock.

"What can I do for you, Araweeta?" My voice was stodgy, disdainful. Even I could hear the note of impatience for this man who had warmly welcomed me into his family's remote village. His father certainly wasn't pleased by my intrusion. But something about the innocent, boyish way Araweeta wore his virility made me very uncomfortable.

"My chil', she missin', docta. She only..." he said, his accent thick, before pausing for a moment in thought, "six-tee-foor luna' cycles old." He pointed to the sky, then glanced hopefully back at me.

Doing some quick math in my head, I concluded his daughter was approximately five years old. I thought I remembered seeing her around the camp—a pretty child with dark hair and bright blue eyes —an anomaly in this part of the world. "What's her name?"

"Pishka."

"I had planned to do some field exploration at Wirta Pata today. I will leave in ten minutes and search for your daughter there."

"Değerli gayretleriniz için teşekkür ederim!" Araweeta nodded his head and stepped back, bowing to me.

I didn't understand the Yine language, but given the context clues, I deduced that Araweeta was grateful and offering his thanks.

I hurried back into the tent to change clothes and prepare for a day spent alone in the Amazonian jungle. While packing my supplies, a realization took hold...one which sent icy shards of dread through my core. Goosebumps lined my skin, despite the brutal heat.

Though young and brawny, I'd recognized something unnerving in Araweeta's eyes while we spoke. Something very much like fear.

———

I had no intention of looking for the girl.

A missing child in this wretched part of the world meant nothing more to me than the goddamn blasted mosquitoes.

Speaking of the mosquitoes...

Fuckers would not leave me alone. At this rate, I'd be bloodless by the time I reached my destination. Repellent sprays were useless, particularly when the mosquitoes were the size of houseflies.

Sighing, I trudged through the thick, green foliage.

I'd been stationed on the Madre de Dios River for the past two weeks. Three short months ago, word had trickled into Sigma Pharmaceuticals—the research facility where I worked as head of the entomology department—that a possible new species of tarantula had been discovered—a tarantula with some unusual behaviors and abilities. The email was so ludicrous, it was easily dismissed. It wasn't until a month ago, when we received a very convincing video clip of this tarantula species in action, that the arachnology team couldn't get my fat ass to Peru fast enough.

So far, I'd been unable to find the arachnid I was searching for, which was unfortunate. And peculiar. The video sent to us was thoroughly investigated, and our tech team concluded it was filmed in and around the very camp where I was currently residing. Despite his obvious attempt at playing dumb, Araweeta knew about the species I'd described—maybe even about the video itself. I couldn't understand the secrecy and lack of forthcoming information, but it was fine. I'd figure it all out. I, after all, had more intelligence in my little toe than all these goddamned jungle freaks combined.

Huffing and puffing through the canopies of lush emerald flora, I glanced at my compass and verified I was still heading in the right direction. Terrified screams echoed through the trees, causing me to jump and get low to the ground, while defensively hunkering my shoulders. I nervously scanned the area for potential threats. Twenty feet above my head, a boa constrictor with a juvenile capybara in its grip, slowly suffocated the weakening rodent, its once shrill screams reduced to gasping squeals.

Seconds later, they too were cut off.

This was hell on earth. A fucking nightmare at every turn.

Shaking my head in contempt, I trudged on—but not before pulling out the machete holstered on my hip.

———

The waters of Wirta Pata lake were displayed before me, its gently lapping waves a deep, dark indigo—the kind of water that held secrets. Centuries worth. The lake bordered the base of Wirta Pata mountain, home to a genus of terrestrial tarantula called *Euathlus*, one of the few high-elevation tarantulas. The *E. truculentus* was easily identifiable by its neon purple femurs, a trait we'd noticed on the tarantula in the video. Yet, that tarantula was most certainly *not* an *E. truculentus*...and the things it did were...well...

No time to think about that.

What I had seen terrified me. I'd assigned an underling to go to South America on my behalf, but Rosalie, my boss and occasional lover, insisted I was the only one who could handle the escalating situation. Until we knew exactly what we were dealing with, she wanted only her best on location. Understandable, but...

...I just needed to find the damn spider. I was desperate to leave this cesspit and return safely to Duluth. A place where nearly everyone was 'Minnesota nice,' and flannel was the epitome of high fashion.

I circled the western-most section of the lake, where the slope of the land gently rose, and rocks of various sizes littered the ground.

Headlamp in place, I donned a pair of thick, elbow-length gloves with elastic cuffs. Carrying a long-handled, spoon-shaped, metal tool in one hand and a large plastic container in the other, I slid rocks around with my foot, looking for burrows. Fifteen minutes in, I was already spent. Deep breaths were hard to come by in such a humid climate... like trying to breathe underwater. The mosquitoes, adept at finding their way beneath my clothes, were even worse by the lake. A feat I didn't think possible.

Unwilling to rest on a rock that might be hiding venomous snakes or spiders, I dropped my decidedly moist body onto a thick patch of dark green grass, shaded by the sturdy trunks of giant bamboo. I'd give myself ten minutes, then resume the search. I'd discovered a kick-ass game on my phone that didn't require the internet—*Plague Inc*. The goal was to infect as many people as I could with my chosen plague, before they found a cure. Morbid but fun.

Twenty minutes later, I was so absorbed in enslaving the world's population with the Neurax worm, I barely registered the quiet giggles, or the pitter-patter of tiny feet, coming toward me. When a delicate hand touched my shoulder, I screamed in surprise, crab-walking backward as fast as my out-of-shape body would allow, before realizing it was just Pishka, Araweeta's daughter. She stood solemnly before me, a tiny thing, probably no more than three feet tall and thirty-five pounds, her long brown hair tangled and full of twigs and leaves.

Probably lice too. Such a filthy, disgusting little girl. Why would Araweeta even want this naughty urchin back?

The cargo shorts she wore were several sizes too big, probably hand-me-downs from other village-children, and her white tank-top was a road map of dirt and stains. Scratches and bruises covered her bare feet and legs, and blood dripped from hands. Yet, she just stood there, gap-toothed smile painted unnaturally across her face.

It occurred to me the situation could work in my favor. If I rescued his precious daughter, it might be enough to convince Araweeta to tell me what he knew, but I needed her to trust me.

Knowing she wouldn't understand a word I was saying, I rambled on in soft, soothing tones, assuring her she'd be 'home in a jiffy.' That she'd be fine once she was back with her family. That I had food and water. That my phone contained fun games she could play.

But Pishka didn't move a muscle. Not even to blink.

I moved closer to show her my phone. *All kids like games, right?* As I nestled beside her, trying to ignore the overwhelming stench emanating from her small frame, she saw the parasitic worms flittering across the screen and giggled. The giggles turned to laughter. She laughed so hard, tears drenched her dirty cheeks. Tears that turned crimson red at the same moment her laughter became piercing screams.

Fearing some deadly jungle virus like Ebola, I'm not ashamed to admit that I ran. I was there to find a tarantula—not deal with primitive medical bullshit. I glanced back and saw she was following. Quickly. She uttered no words—not that I would have understood them anyway. Just glared at me with her blood-streaked face, a maniacal look in those oddly out-of-place sapphire eyes.

A few minutes later, my body was fried. The heat, the dehydration, the rapid build-up of lactic acid in my muscles...I tripped over a tree root and didn't get up.

I couldn't.

But I wanted to.

Pishka scared the ever-loving shit out of me. Something was terribly wrong with the child, and I suspected I knew just what it was.

Staying as still as I could, I attempted to catch my breath, hoping she'd be so focused on the path before her, she'd run right past me. My only wish was to get back to my too-warm tent, curl up, and sleep for days. I risked lifting my head, covertly scanning the area. She was thirty feet to my right, standing atop a large rock...staring directly at me. Her once blue eyes were now a soulless black—*what the ever-loving fuck?*—the sclera red with broken capillaries.

I tried to stand, but my legs were unresponsive lumps. The

pounding inside my chest was so hard and fast, I believed I was having a heart attack...an unsurprising turn of events, given my family history.

As Pishka raced toward me, I swore to myself, and to whatever god or goddess might be listening, that I'd start a diet and exercise regimen as soon as I was stateside. If only I could survive one encounter with this rabid jungle brat. Closing my eyes, I fully expected to feel her to tear out my tongue...or maybe rip into my neck with her baby teeth. She did neither. Instead, she gently rubbed her fingers through my hair...

...and then vomited a thick, bloody mixture across my face.

CHAPTER 1
BETHANY

How big is this guy's prostate, anyway?

I sighed discreetly, attempting to maneuver the foley catheter through the mostly obstructed entrance into his bladder. When it had painfully coiled up inside him for the second time, and he'd called me a 'dumb bitch' at least twice as many times before throwing an empty emesis basin at my head, I gave up and notified the doctor.

"Fine. I didn't figure you'd get it in anyway," she responded over the phone.

I paused, allowing the information to percolate. *So, you just had me torture the poor man for shits and giggles? I hope one of these days when you're old, you get to endure a foley catheter coiled up inside your...*

Her voice interrupted. "Just make sure he's kept on strict fluid restrictions, and I'll see him tomorrow."

The dial tone sounded in my ear.

I hung up, staring morosely at the receiver before glancing at the clock hanging on the wall. Three hours. Just three short hours until I ditched this joint and began my four-day weekend. Maybe I'd stop at that new Ethiopian restaurant on the way home, then treat myself to a 'Shudder and chill' kinda night.

Yep. That'll do nicely. And if I can't find anything worth watching on Shudder, the number of unread books on my Kindle has become laughable. What was it that one horror author said? The funny one? 'I know I'll die one day, but I buy books like an immortal.' Smart guy.

I walked toward the nurses' station, small smile playing upon my lips, happy with my plans.

Dee, the charge nurse, addressed me impassively. "Bethany, a new patient is being admitted. I don't have all the details yet, but since you discharged Mrs. Childress earlier, this one's yours."

Fuck.

"Yeah, okay," I said. "ETA?"

"Don't know."

"Diagnosis?"

"Don't know." She nonchalantly shrugged her bony shoulders, a not-so-subtle smirk etched across her unarguably homely face. "The only thing they told me is the patient is male and in bad shape, but not bad enough for the ICU. It's a full house today, and we're the only floor with beds available, so he's ours."

Calling it now. My final three hours will be a nightmare. I bet my entire paycheck I'll be transferring this dude to ICU before I go home. My earlier excitement vanished. I loved being a nurse, but bullshit hospital politics drove me mad.

"He'll be in room 449." Dee finished writing the patient's last name beside his room number on the dry-erase board, then turned toward me and winked. "They did say he's noisy, so I'm putting him at the end of the hallway. Hopefully he won't bother the other patients there."

"Awesome. Thanks," I said, voice flat. "Let me know when..." I looked at the board, "...Mr. Delgado gets here."

"It's 'doctor.'"

"What?"

"He's Dr. Delgado. Oh, and I'm guessing you'll know he's arrived without me ever saying a word." The smirk was back.

If *I* were a doctor, I'd diagnose Dee with stage four *bitchitis*. The woman was just plain awful. We'd gone to nursing school together—had been roommates our junior and senior years. Because she'd preferred fucking guys—*all* the guys—to studying, she'd nearly flunked out. Oddly, she blamed me for her shortcomings, a stance I hadn't understood until a psychiatrist, who I'd worked with on the mental health floor, joined me for lunch one day. He'd seen the way she treated me, watched her overly dramatic behavior, the entitlement and self-absorbed egocentrism. He'd observed her lack of empathy and the constant need for attention and praise.

"Must be hard dealing with a histrionic narcissist every day," he'd said when I mentioned Dee. I'd kept my mouth shut, not wanting to fan the flames. Later that night, as soon as I arrived home, I Googled the diagnosis. What I learned explained so much about my relationship with Dee.

That we not only worked in the same hospital, but on the same floor was a freaky—and entirely unpleasant—-coincidence. And, because she was a groveling ass-kisser, she'd been promoted to charge nurse before more deserving nurses, including myself. It gave her the power to make my shifts indescribably miserable. To protect myself, I made sure we worked opposite weekends. Even still, I occasionally had to put up with her mean-girl bullshit.

Like now.

Dee knew damn well the next patient admission should be Tony's. He only had four patients. I had five. But, whatever. I'd do what I needed to do, then leave this place for four glorious, self-indulgent days. Hell, maybe I'd finally open the wand vibrator I'd dropped fifty bucks on a couple weeks ago and give it a test run. I desperately needed physical release, and boyfriends were overrated.

But what about girlfriends?

I blushed just thinking about hooking up with a woman. I'd never considered myself a lesbian...or even bisexual. Yet one night, bored and inebriated on cheap wine, I'd found some female escorts on-line that—for lack of a better description—were scorching hot. Also, confession time...I *was* curious about grinding against the soft wetness of a female partner.

Would it feel like rubbing against my pillow? Or...better?

Definitely something to think about.

I squeezed my thighs together to quell the throbbing button between them. As turned on as I suddenly was, I couldn't help but wish I was riding a pretty face with a tornado-tongue...

Stifling another frustrated sigh, I checked on my patients, then visited the nurse's lounge for some downtime before my mystery patient arrived. Michelle was lying on the couch, eyes closed, giant headphones covering her ears.

I couldn't help myself. I ogled.

She was beautiful. Wide-set brown eyes. Wavy, espresso-colored hair with caramel highlights that fell to perfectly shaped breasts. Soft, plump lips that simply begged to surround my nipples and suck....

Fucking hell, what is wrong *with me today? She's my* co-worker, *for crying out loud.*

My libido was clearly cranked up to combustible. I squirmed uncomfortably.

"Hey, Bethany." Michelle had removed her headphones and was now sitting...watching me. "Everything okay?"

"Yep! I mean, yes, everything is fine." I forced a chuckle. "You caught me daydreaming."

Her expression was knowing as she strode gracefully across the room. "Hope it was a good one," she said, placing the headphones inside her locker.

"Better than good." I smiled half-heartedly.

She slammed the door shut, turned, and looked at me. *Really* looked.

"I have those *better than good* daydreams every once in a while, myself." She gave me an adorable wink, then, seemingly deciding something, walked toward me.

I couldn't look at her.

"Maybe we should hang out this weekend," she finally said. "I know we both have a few days off."

"I'd like that," I managed to stammer as goosebumps pimpled my skin.

"Cool." She handed me her phone. "Give me your info."

My hands shook as I typed my number into her phone and gave it back. Seconds later, my cell beeped with an incoming text message.

"Now you have my info too." She smiled, and I couldn't help noticing her perfect teeth, and the small dimple in her left cheek. "I'll call you later tonight to make plans."

"I...I'll look forward to it."

Michelle waved as she pushed open the door and exited into the hallway.

Is she wanting to hang out as friends, or did she just ask me on a date? Maybe a booty call?

There wasn't time to dissect the conversation now, but I sure would when I got home this evening.

Feeling daring—and oddly drunk after making unexpected plans with Michelle—I poured myself a cup of coffee from the lounge carafe. It tasted like ass sludge. I suspected it had been made around the same time "Girls Just Want to Have Fun" was popular on the radio. As I poured the ebony liquid down the sink drain, I startled upon hearing a banshee-like shriek coming from the vicinity of the patient elevators.

Yikes! Is a coyote on the loose?

I went hesitantly toward the noise and commotion. Dee saw me coming and motioned with her hand, while speaking to the man standing beside her. His expression was comically grim. Hers was smug.

"I'm Bethany," I said, glancing at the writhing figure lying on the gurney. Broken blood vessels crisscrossed his skin, giving it a zombie-like appearance. His eyes appeared as though the orbs themselves were bleeding. *Oh yeah. He'll be going to the ICU within the hour.* "Mister..." I caught myself. "*Dr.* Delgado is my patient."

The man offered a tight smile. "Hi, Bethany. I'm Alex from the ER. Care to show us to room 449?" He unlocked the brake on Dr. Delgado's gurney and grabbed the headboard, pushing it expertly toward me. Dee remained uncharacteristically quiet.

"Sure," I said. "No problem. Follow me." I led him to the far end of the hallway and opened a door on the left. "Here we go, Dr. Delgado. Your home away from home." He groaned in response.

After we'd transferred him to the stationary bed, I got his IV fluids set up on a pump, while Alex re-tied his four-point restraints.

"Does he actually need those?" I hated restraining patients. Unfortunately, it was sometimes necessary for both their safety and mine.

"Completely." Alex looked pointedly at me. "Want to step outside so I can fill you in?"

"Sure," I said. "Just give me a minute." He nodded and left the room.

Giving Dr. Delgado one final check to ensure he would stay safe while I was otherwise distracted, I lifted the blanket to make sure the foley catheter wasn't kinked and noted his hugely distended abdomen.

He was a hefty man, but this...this was not fat. Mystified and vaguely repulsed by the gestational-looking belly on the good doctor, I placed my hands against his feverish skin and palpated. It was... squishy. Like a waterbed.

Is he in liver failure? Is this ascites? It would certainly explain his confusion.

Something moved inside him.

A gentle shift that felt intentional. Somehow...alive. I stepped away from the bed, my breath caught in my throat. A small lump protruded an inch above his belly button, moved back and forth as though waving hello, then disappeared just as quickly.

Delgado's restrained hand grabbed mine. A sweaty, grimy hand with dark, viscous blood sunk deep into the crevices of otherwise clean fingernails. I tried to pull away, but the grip was firm. He glared at me, crying bloody tears of rage.

"Get it out, you dog-fucking bitch! Now! Do you hear me? Get this goddamn thing out of my guts!" Delgado's face was an angry red. Purple, knot-like veins protruded from his forehead. His brown eyes were glassy and crazed. "Help me, you rotten cunt! For Christ's sake, *help me!*" His words turned into demented shrieking. The bed shook beneath his thrashing body.

"Dr. Delgado...that's no way to speak to somebody who is trying to help you!" I was trying to keep my cool, because he was obviously very ill, but *damn*. A dog-fucking bitch?

Alex was suddenly beside me, jerking the man's hand from mine. My body shuddered in relief as I was freed from the scorching, gore-coated claw. "I need to talk to your nurse for a moment," he informed the doctor. "Try to stay calm."

Without waiting for a response, he turned and exited. Refusing to look at my patient this time, I followed Alex to a charting nook three doors down from Dr. Delgado's room. I plopped into a chair and let out a long, quivering breath.

"What the hell is wrong with him?" My voice was raw. "I've been doing this nursing thing for a while now, but there is something very *horribly* amiss with that man. Something I'm not sure I have the skills to care for. Hell, something I'm not sure *any* of us have the skills to care for! I know this is going to sound crazy, but I swear I saw it. His abdomen, it was...it was *moving*."

Alex sat with his head down, his hands torpedoing his hair in multiple directions. "Yeah, I know. I saw some stuff too."

I leaned forward. "What?"

He didn't respond.

"Goddammit, what did you see?" I couldn't stop thinking of that little protrusion popping out of Dr. Delgado's belly...like a baby's hand or knee late in a woman's pregnancy. The revulsion was so great, I shuddered.

When he finally spoke, his voice was a nervous whisper. "The doctors saw something on the CT scan they didn't like, but from what I could tell, they had no idea what it was. Their best guess was a tumor, but the radiologist told me privately it looked like—" He hesitated, looking behind him and leaning in before continuing, "He said whatever it was appeared to be covered in hair."

"A teratoma?" I asked, referring to rare tumors made from tissue, hair, teeth, and various other body parts.

"I asked the same thing. He was positive it wasn't a teratoma, but then—" He let out a slightly hysterical laugh. "I saw something else."

"Okay."

He rubbed his hands over his face. When he looked at me, his eyes were nearly as crazed as Delgado's. "You're not going to believe me. Hell, I don't believe it myself." He snorted. "I'm questioning everything I saw."

"Do me a favor and start at the beginning," I said softly. "I wasn't given any information at all from Dee. Before we get to the outlandish, let's do the Nursing 101 thing, okay?"

"Good idea. Let's do that."

I took notes as he talked. "The patient, Francisco Delgado, a fifty-six-year-old male, was brought into the ER around noon today, vomiting copious amounts of blood. He was alert to person, place, and time when he arrived and informed us he'd been in the Amazonian jungle for the past three weeks doing research. Obviously, that immediately put us on alert for one of the hemorrhagic fevers, but he said he'd been tested for all of them while he was still there, a standard protocol required by his job, and the results were negative. He even showed us the documentation, though we still called the lab and verified the information. Everything checked out.

We did the standard blood work, most of which wasn't remarkable. As expected, given his symptoms, the clotting factors were abnormal, and the WBCs were slightly elevated, though his eosinophils were off-the-charts high. Electrolytes were out of range, though not grossly so. Kidney and liver function were about the same as they were at his last annual check-up. He does have a fatty liver but is on medication. Chest x-ray was within normal limits. EKG had a few PVCs, but nothing serious. As you probably saw from his catheter, he has hematuria."

I nodded, recalling the blood-filled, burgundy-tinted urine flowing into the drain bag.

Alex went on. "During his time in the ER, blood vessels in his eyes and beneath his skin started rupturing. The doctors weren't concerned, having ruled out the hemorrhagic viruses. They all agreed it was from projectile vomiting and aggressive muscle contractions. But then the pain started, and with that, his mental status deteriorated. He was babbling nonsense about the jungle, seeing things that weren't there, scaring the other patients with his screaming. I gave him some Valium, but it didn't do a damn thing. At one point, he pulled me aside and told me something about a little demon girl in the jungle who puked in his mouth...and a lake with secrets...and..." Alex's face turned pink with embarrassment, "...something about a horse cock."

"Jesus," I whispered.

"I called his place of employment, here in Duluth. It's some sort of medical research facility. Anyway, they told me that one week ago, he'd been found beside a mountain lake, propped against some bamboo, soaking wet, and babbling incoherently. Blood was found on surrounding leaves and rocks, but Delgado had no obvious injuries. The tribesman who found him has a missing daughter who, as far as we know, is still lost." Alex took a deep breath and continued. "He was transported to the nearest city, where they did all the appropriate testing before bringing him back to the states, like I mentioned. He arrived in Minnesota yesterday."

"So...did he see the missing child? Did he *do* something to her? Was it her blood? Could she be in the lake?"

Alex shrugged. "Your guess is as good as mine, Bethany. I'm just relaying the information I was given."

"This is freaking me out."

"I get it. It's a highly unusual case."

I drew a smiley face on my patient notes, trying to lighten my mood. Even it looked frightened. "Continue, please."

"I was on the phone with the radiologist, discussing his CT scan results, when Delgado suddenly went silent. Worried he might've passed away, I told the doc I'd call him back and went to his bedside. The constant chatter and screaming had completely ceased. I couldn't get him to respond to me. He just stared blankly at the wall. And—" Alex swallowed hard.

"And?"

"And that's when I saw something come out of his ear. It was long, segmented, hairy, and had a purplish sheen."

"What the hell was it?" I was horrified.

"I think...I think it was a spider's leg." He swallowed. "A big one."

I laughed. "Oh, come on! A spider?"

"He's the head of entomology at this research facility I mentioned."

"Yeah? So what? That doesn't mean he has a giant spider living inside him."

"His specialty is arachnids."

I choked on the sip of water I'd just taken.

"I couldn't get Sigma, his employer, to tell me why he was in Peru. Apparently, it was some top-secret mission. But why would they urgently send an overweight, middle-aged researcher, one who specializes in arachnids, to a remote Amazonian jungle?"

"Fine. Fine. Let's say there is a spider inside his body. A large one. What the hell do we do? Are we in danger?"

"I mentioned the possibility to his team of doctors, and they all looked at me like I had two heads. I mean, for Christ's sake, just because nothing with eight legs showed up on his scans, doesn't mean it's not in there."

"Again, what do we do?"

"I think we keep him away from everyone we can. We can't trust that he's safe. His diagnosis is acute hemorrhagic gastroenteritis, and the plan is to give him fluids, IV Protonix, and treat his pain until he's stable enough to be sent home."

I shook my head in disbelief.

"C'mon, Bethany. You know how ER docs are. Slap a diagnosis on them, write a few instructions, and send them on their way."

"But how can they just ignore—"

"Once they're admitted, they're another doctor's problem."

"Healthcare in 'Merica," I said gravely, not disputing his claim.

"Yep." He stood. "When does your shift end?"

I looked at my Apple watch. "In about two hours."

"Shit. Me too." He glanced up and down the hallway, then turned back to me. "Do everything you can to get him to the ICU. He'll be more isolated there...far fewer people coming and going. I tried like hell to get him sent there, but his doctors refused to believe he was sick enough."

"I'll do my best, but if they wouldn't take him thirty minutes ago, I doubt they'll take him now."

"His condition is deteriorating rapidly. Just keep an eye on him."

"Of course I will. He *is* my patient. I'm just a little leery—"

A piercing scream—*female*—echoed throughout the hallway.

"What now?" Alex asked, running toward Delgado's room.

Throwing open the door, we found my nursing assistant, Trudy, covered in blood and green bile. She was sobbing and pointing at the patient.

"I just—" She shook her head and lifted her hands in despair. "What the *actual* fuck?"

I didn't respond. I couldn't. What we saw defied all medical logic.

Dr. Delgado looked jubilant. A too-large smile was pasted across his pale, diaphoretic face. This, despite the deep crevices zigzagging across his skin. They were dry. Dark. Scabby. And were those—I leaned closer—*hairs?*

Diaphanous white threads floated through the air surrounding him. I moved closer, and Trudy screamed. "Don't! They're pure acid! They burned me."

I turned to the poor girl covered in Dr. Delgado's gastric fluids. "What do you mean they burned you?"

"A piece sizzled through my skin like it was warm butter!" She held out her arm, and I saw a large, weeping gash.

"Oh my God, Trudy! We need to get you to the emergency room. That's deep!" But before I could lead her out of the room, Alex stopped me.

"Bethany, something is going on with Delgado. Call a code. Now!"

I did as I was told, then ran back into the room. Pulpy, gray mush oozed from Dr. Delgado's nose as Alex performed aggressive CPR.

"What happened?"

"I'm not sure. He seemed to have a small seizure and stopped breathing. Then this...stuff started coming out of his head."

As the code team entered, I noticed Trudy, wiping gore from her face, slip outside the room.

CHAPTER 2
ALEX

A piece of white thread—webbing?—landed on my hand as I began chest compressions, causing the skin to burn and sizzle. Blood-filled blisters formed. It hurt like hell, but I brushed it away and kept working, knowing a man's life was at stake. I'd deal with my injury later. Delgado was an asshole, but he was also a very sick man. I'd do whatever I could to save him. It was my job.

The code team arrived with the crash cart. Less than a minute later, Delgado was intubated and hooked to an electrocardiogram machine which monitored his heart rhythms. Bethany placed adhesive pads on his chest and side to prepare for defibrillation. I stopped chest compressions only when they shocked him, stepping away from the metal framed bed, to not get a jolt myself. He was in ventricular fibrillation, a dangerous arrhythmia caused by the heart's ventricles contracting rapidly and in uncoordinated movements, preventing blood from getting to the rest of his body. If we couldn't convert the rhythm to a more manageable one, Delgado would die.

"Clear!" Dr. Reznik, the physician running the code, shouted. The entire team stepped away from the bed as she placed the defibrillator paddles against the adhesive pads, then depressed the button. Two-hundred-fifty joules of electricity shot through Delgado's three-hundred-pound body, causing the muscles throughout to contract. "Jesus, he has so much fluid on him, his intra-abdominal pressure must be through the roof! The epinephrine drip is going, right?"

"Yes," Bethany said, checking the bag. "Dosage is one milligram per hundred milliliters."

"Okay, let's speed up the drip and give him some amiodarone, three hundred milligrams. Quick push!"

As I resumed chest compressions, my hand landed on a thick, purple hair protruding from the scabby crevices zigzagging across Delgado's body. "Goddammit!" I muttered as it penetrated my skin.

"What's wrong?" Dr. Reznik asked.

A deep itching sensation, a thousand times worse than a mosquito bite, spread throughout my hand. "Nothing, doc," I said, massaging my palm. "Just these damn hairs. What the hell are they?"

"I'm not sure," she answered. "I've never seen anything like them."

Chest compressions were nearly impossible with the deep-rooted itch in my hand. "Need a replacement," I yelled. Another nurse took over, while Bethany continued administering the intravenous medications ordered by Dr. Reznik.

Delgado's cardiac rhythm devolved into a grouping of unidentifiable squiggles across the monitor's screen.

"We're losing him!" Reznik shouted. "Let's get epinephrine five milligrams, atropine one milligram, and a thousand of calcium chloride pushed stat!"

I'd planned to help Bethany draw up the medications, but the itching in my hand was maddening. I could focus on nothing else. My palm was cherry red and covered in a fine rash.

"I'm calling it," I heard Dr. Reznik say moments later. She glanced at the utilitarian white clock hanging on the wall. "Six-fourteen p.m."

Energy vacated the room as quickly as it entered. The entire medical team looked deflated.

"Bethany, he's your patient?" Not looking away from Delgado's body, Bethany nodded. "Okay. I'll leave the paperwork for you at the front desk. Page me with the number of his next of kin...or if you need anything else."

When Bethany failed to respond, I said, "Thanks, Dr. Reznik. I'd just brought Dr. Delgado up from the ER, so I'll stay and help her get all this sorted out. I've been with him all afternoon and know more about him than she does. This was...unexpected."

"Aren't they always?" Dr. Reznik said, chucking her gloves into the trash and hurrying down the hallway.

As the room cleared, Bethany remained by Delgado's side. I knew why. "Any movement?" I asked, joining her at the bedside.

"Nothing." She sounded almost...disappointed.

"Okay. I'm going to check his chart and find out who needs to be notified. I'll be back."

Three seconds later, "Oh my God! Alex, look!"

Dr. Delgado's body was gyrating, the rictus grin still etched across his fleshy face. The scabby wounds crisscrossing his skin had split open and were oozing blue-tinted liquid.

"What the hell is that?"

"So—" she seemed embarrassed. "Arachnids don't have hemoglobin. Their blood looks blue."

"Okay." That was a little freaky. "And tarantulas are covered in hair, right?"

"Yep." She nodded. "Many of them use that hair as a defense mechanism, shooting it at their predators. It can cause an intense itch."

"You're telling me. This itches like a motherfucker." I showed her my hand.

"We need to get that treated."

"Not now," I said, pointing to Dr. Delgado, whose body had gone still. "Let's get him into a body bag and contain whatever the hell is hiding inside him."

"Yeah." she said wearily. "Good idea."

"Think we should put some protective garb on first?"

"An even better idea. I'll get the body bag, you grab some gowns, masks...whatever you think we'll need."

We left the room, closing the door behind us.

CHAPTER 3

TRUDY

I couldn't stand the stench coating my body. I needed to wash off and change my scrubs. While everyone was distracted, I left the freak's room and made my way to the staff lounge. In addition to our lockers, it also housed a small bathroom with a shower for staff working doubles, or for those, like me, who desperately needed to wash off putrid body fluids.

Momma tried to tell me that 'wiping smelly asses and giving bed baths' was for girls far less pretty than myself, but I had a daughter to feed and clothe. Being a CNA gave me job security. Plus, I was good at what I did. I enjoyed talking to the patients, and I always did my best to help the nurses in any way I could. I knew how busy they got...how much was thrown at them throughout every shift they worked.

When Dee told me I needed to get baseline vital signs on Bethany's new patient, I happily obliged. Bethany was my favorite nurse. She was funny and sarcastic and kind and did her very best for her patients. Everyone loved her. Which was why the animosity I sensed between her and Dee was so surprising.

Their bad energy was so thick and noxious, it sucked the oxygen right out of a room. Without knowing their history, all of us—everyone working on our floor—intuitively knew it was Dee's fault. Because Dee was a sour, hateful bitch.

I looked at my reflection in the mirror and cringed. I'd been shit on, pissed on, vomited on, spit on...and one patient had even pulled some of my hair out. I took it all in stride because the people who'd done these things were sick. In most cases, they had no control over their bodily functions...and if they did, they didn't always have the mental capacity to know better. It came with the territory, and I accepted that.

But Dr. Delgado...

He'd *told* me what he was going to do and laughed maniacally when he did. All this after informing me I looked like a 'pig's droopy ball sack.' I didn't get a chance to tell him what I thought *he* looked like, because that's when he grabbed my arm and vomited what felt like twenty gallons of blood on my head.

Looking more closely, I noticed small white globules stuck in my hair too.

Yuck. What is that?

Maybe he had some sort of hyperlipidemia issue, and they were fat globules? He certainly looked the type to have elevated cholesterol levels. Eh. He'd probably just eaten at Long John Silver's. I snort-laughed.

The fan in the lavatory rattled to life, startling me, and causing the rotten, digestive juice aroma to permeate the room. The smell, combined with the memory of that repulsive funk splattering into my mouth, had me rushing to the toilet and purging the contents of my own sickened stomach.

I knew I needed to talk to the infectious disease team to start post-exposure prophylaxis, but right now, I just wanted to get cleaned up. I rinsed out my eyes, nose, and mouth with tap water from the sink, then threw my contaminated scrubs into the biohazard laundry bag conveniently placed beside the shower. Adjusting the water to near scalding, I entered the stall and closed the door behind me. There was shampoo, conditioner, and body wash mounted to the wall. I pumped out some of the eucalyptus-scented shampoo and rubbed it onto my scalp. The lather was minimal. I knew my hair would look dull and lank after using the cheap hospital products, but dull and lank was a vast improvement over bloody and fetid.

Closing my eyes, I let the hot water stream over my face. My body was oddly achy and sore, though I couldn't recall doing anything to have caused those symptoms. Still, I enjoyed the massaging sensation of the water. Though the hospital cheaped-out on toiletries, the shower head provided a powerful flow...the perfect way to relax the muscles and clear the mind. Pink water circled the drain. Dr. Delgado's blood mercifully washed away forever.

Finally feeling squeaky clean, I stepped onto the white bathmat. Everything in the hospital was white. Easier to bleach out stains. Grabbing a towel from a stack folded neatly on a shelf, I dried my face.

Red streaks marred the towel's nubby surface.

"Shit. Did I miss a spot?" A drop of blood hit the bathmat. "How in the heck did I stay in the shower for ten minutes and not get clean?"

I hopped back in for another thorough cleansing, utilizing more of the sharp, slightly astringent body wash. After one final rinse, I turned off the water.

Dee was gonna be pissed I'd been missing for so long. Oh, well. "'Tough titty,' said the kitty," I murmured, snort-laughing again. Though terribly unsexy, snorting was becoming my thing. *Or maybe it's your way of rationalizing a big, scary fucking deal.*

Sighing, I stepped out of the shower, glimpsing myself in the steamy mirror. I stared incomprehensibly as my nipples dripped dark —almost black—blood. My long blonde hair was painted red from oozing follicles. In that heart-stopping moment, I realized...

It wasn't Delgado's blood.

It was mine.

CHAPTER 4

BETHANY

After wrestling Dr. Delgado into the body bag, I dressed Alex's hand wound and treated his rash, before venturing to the nurse's desk. Dr. Reznik cursed quietly and hung up the phone.

"Oh, Bethany, I'm glad I caught you. I just tried calling Rosalie Dowd, the contact person on Dr. Delgado's chart. It was...strange."

"How so?" I asked.

"When I told her he'd passed away, and we weren't sure why, she hung up without saying a word. Maybe it was shock, maybe grief, but I've never had anyone react that way before."

"Yeah," I nodded. "Definitely weird."

"This whole case is peculiar as fuck," Alex said, voice terse.

"What do you mean?" Dr. Reznik asked, curiosity piqued. "Seemed like a routine code to me."

Before Alex could say anything more, I jumped in. "Alex has been with Delgado in the ER all afternoon. I think he's shocked by how quickly the doctor went downhill."

"Ah." Dr. Reznik nodded knowingly. "Well, it happens that way sometimes. Human bodies are full of secrets. It's our job to expose them."

"They sure are," I said, thinking about Delgado's disconcerting abdominal protrusion. I was certain I didn't want to expose whatever *that* was.

"All right, I have more patients to see, so I'm heading off. Page me if you need anything else."

"Thanks. Will do."

Alex sat at the desk, charting the events that had transpired the past couple hours, while I made rounds on the rest of my patients. As I drained amber-colored urine from a catheter bag to measure Mr. Casper's output, I sighed.

My libido had vacated the building.

CHAPTER 5
TRUDY

Smiling happily, I made my way to Dr. Delgado's room. The two of us needed to talk.

I'd tucked my slimy hair beneath a baseball cap I found in an open locker, slipped on a pair of sunglasses I'd found in a neighboring one, and wrapped an ACE bandage around my breasts to prevent oozing.

It wasn't working.

I was a leaky faucet, blood dripping from every orifice. But I didn't care. I felt great...better than ever! And I had things to do, people to see. Maybe even my daughter, if I could get to the little bitch.

I was thankful the hallway was empty. Anyone who saw me would be far more concerned about my 'affliction' than I was.

My movements were twitchy and spasmodic as I opened the door to his private room. Giggling, I unzipped the black body bag.

Did Bethany really think this would work?

I stripped off the already stained scrubs, leaving them wadded on the floor beside the bed. Crawling inside the vinyl bag, I purred like a cat as my warm nakedness pressed against Delgado's unyielding coolness. The blue blood lining the body bag soaked into my skin, making me feel alive. Invincible.

This wasn't about sex...but I wanted it to be. I needed this man. Needed to dominate his corpse.

As if he could read my thoughts—and he probably could—his cock slowly rose.

"That's it, baby. Come to mama," I said, massaging his balls.

I straddled his body, taking his—surprisingly small, given his overall size—erection inside me. As I thrashed against him, a hair-covered, segmented leg extended from my anus—I somehow knew, even though I couldn't see it—and groped for the hair-covered, segmented leg extending from his. When they joined, a jolt of electricity coursed through my already aroused body. My purpose became clear.

Just before we climaxed together.

CHAPTER 6

MICHELLE

I finished a round of tedious charting, checked on my patients, then headed to the staff lounge for a break. I'd been distracted the past few hours, thinking about Bethany and the way she'd looked at me earlier. Every indication led me to believe my attraction was reciprocated, though I suspected that, unlike me, she wasn't a lesbian...just curious.

I'd had my share of heartbreak in the past, making me far more cautious in my current relationships. Though I'd once enjoyed booty calls, I now avoided the Katy Perry 'kissed a girl and liked it' types. The girls who yearned only for the experience. Who would one day brag to their heterosexual partners, "Of course I've been with a woman," just to seem naughtier and more desirable.

I was so much more than a plaything for some rando sowing her wild oats. I was a woman with feelings, desires, and dreams. Yet, there was Bethany, her blonde hair pulled forever into a messy-as-crap ponytail, no makeup except for clear Chapstick, her only jewelry a gold pug necklace she never took off...and I really liked her. She was unapologetically real and somehow vulnerable. I'd suspected for a while she was struggling with her identity—sexual, and other-

33

wise—who she was, what she needed to be happy, and what she wanted from this batshit circus we called life. Maybe she'd finally figured it out...and maybe, if I was lucky, she'd offer me a starring role in her show.

I hoped so.

Bethany was an excellent nurse...kind, caring, thorough, knowledgeable. She gave the profession a good name. My shifts were always better when I shared them with her.

I lived just northeast of Duluth in Two Harbors. It was a scenic small town, nestled against the rocky shores of Lake Superior, and I loved living there. Though I could certainly do without the thirty-minute drive.

Maybe a few months from now, Bethany will be making the drive with me. We'll gossip about the other nurses, turn on Sirius radio and sing at the top of our lungs, maybe she'll even put her hand on my thigh as I drive....

A real-life, basic human need spoiled my daydream. Bladder full, I pulled open the door to the bathroom in the staff lounge.

Blood was everywhere. It coated the bathroom floor and was splattered across the walls and ceiling. Smeared, burgundy handprints covered every surface.

I hadn't heard about a staff accident, but clearly something had gone down. Staring at the gory mess, I felt a hand touched my shoulder and jumped, startled.

"Jesus! You scared the shit out of me!"

Bethany gaped in horrified wonder at the state of the bathroom, unable to respond. Alex, a nurse I recognized from the ER, stood protectively behind her. I felt a pang of jealousy.

"Are you...okay?" she finally asked me.

"I'm fine. This isn't my blood."

"I'm guessing Trudy got a shower after Dr. Delgado spewed blood all over her. She disappeared while we were coding him, but she was a total mess."

"Why would she just leave the bathroom in this state though? Doesn't seem like something she'd do."

"No, you're right," Bethany said. "She's usually so organized and efficient. We need to report this to the biohazard clean-up team and find Trudy."

Alex, who had been quiet to that point, added, "She didn't have this much blood on her in Delgado's room. And it was mixed with bile, which I'm not seeing here." He peered more closely. "And what's that gooey, white shit?"

"I hadn't even noticed that!" I said, nose wrinkled in disgust.

"It's not semen, is it?" Bethany asked.

"No. I don't think so. Wrong texture," Alex responded.

"We'll bow to your expertise on that one," I said, wan smile on my face. Bethany chuckled.

"I'll call the clean-up crew," Alex continued, unphased by the joke. "You two find Trudy and make sure she's okay."

"Sounds good." I looked at Bethany. "Ready?" The blush that spread across her cheeks made me smile.

"Let's do it."

I wondered if she'd intended the double entendre.

CHAPTER 7

TRUDY

I pushed open the door.

Two elderly patients were inside, asleep in their beds. I evaluated both. Mr. Olson had a broken hip but was otherwise healthy. Mr. Schmidt was hypertensive, diabetic, and had been on hemodialysis for the past three years.

Coming to a decision, I walked to the man and gently stroked his hair. His eyes opened, face shining with a happy smile.

He knew me.

He liked me.

Most importantly, he trusted me.

And he didn't care that I was wearing a hospital gown saturated with blood.

"Open your mouth, sweetie," I whispered, voice kind. He did so willingly, assuming I was there to moisten his dry lips and apply lip balm, something I'd done dozens of times since his admission.

Instead, I projectile vomited my bleeding guts onto his disgusting, old man face and ventured to the next room, my gown leaving droplets of bright red blood on the white linoleum floors.

CHAPTER 8
BETHANY

"Dee, have you seen Trudy?"

"No, I haven't. I'm not sure where the hell she disappeared to, but if you see her, tell her to report to me immediately. She's in big trouble." She looked at her watch. "And make sure you have everything completed by shift's end, or I'll write you up."

"Don't threaten me, Dee. You know Dr. Delgado's admission and subsequent death put me way behind schedule. We both know he should have gone to the ICU, and now I'm playing catch-up. But first, I need to find Trudy. The staff bathroom looks like the site of a crime scene. I'm worried about her."

"What about the bathroom?" Dee was checked out of our conversation, absorbed in her phone.

"Dr. Delgado puked blood and digestive juices all over her. She took off when he coded, and I assumed the mess in the shower was the result."

That got her attention. "Dammit, Bethany! Why didn't you tell me earlier? You know this is something I must report to management! And Trudy needs immediate treatment in the ER! For Christ's sake, find her!" She vanished into her office, angrily slamming the door behind her.

"I thought saving a patient's life took priority," I mumbled to the closed door.

Michelle joined me, shaking her head. "That woman desperately needs to get laid."

"Don't we all?" I unthinkingly quipped, then flushed with embarrassment.

"Patience, pretty young thing," Michelle said, strolling down the hall, hands clasped innocently behind her back.

I processed her words for several seconds. "Wait, what?" I ran after her.

CHAPTER 9
TRUDY

R oom number 415.

I inhaled the ripe scent of fresh (or maybe not-so-fresh) prey. Problem was, both fellows were in the hospital for the same thing...congestive heart failure.

I sniffed again.

Mr. Cartman was brewing a lymphoma that doctors hadn't yet discovered, and Mr. Casper had new onset emphysema, also undiagnosed.

Hmm. Decisions, decisions.

"Trudy, honey, you okay? What's going on? Let me help you, young lady." Mr. Casper looked both startled and concerned by my appearance.

His roommate was too engrossed in *Jeopardy* to pay attention to the bloody girl standing in the doorway, which made my decision easy.

I grabbed H. Michael Casper by the neck, pried his jaws apart, and upchucked my precious gift into his mouth. By the time he'd gathered his wits and screamed for help, I was halfway down the hallway, a huge smile whittled across my gore-streaked face, lips crusted in jelly-like, maroon clots.

Annoyed by the confines of heavy, wet clothing, I removed the dripping gown and threw it across the hall. It hooked on the corner of an ugly, generic watercolor painting and hung there, dribbling my infested blood onto the poorly executed mountain and the dark, rippling lake. It reminded me of the place where Francisco—now that we were lovers, calling him Delgado seemed cheeky and unsophisticated—had been in Peru. I could see it all as clearly as though I'd been there myself.

Humming to myself, I stepped into the next room.

Ah! Mrs. Jones and Ms. Dahl. Two of my favorites!

They were awake and chatty, the petty gossip stopping mid-sentence as they glimpsed my bloodstained nakedness and gasped in prudish shock. Crimson rivulets were stark against my pale, nearly translucent skin.

"Oh, my Jesus in heaven, hit the call button, Marge! Trudy's been attacked!" Ms. Dahl hurried toward me, the white blanket from her bed gripped tightly inside her hands, intent on covering my shame.

I gave her a hard shove and went straight for Mrs. Jones, who, despite her fragility fighting stage four ovarian cancer, had still managed to hit the call light.

Shit.

"Dear girl, let me help—-"

I punched her face hard enough to knock her out, pushed her back on the bed, held both eyes open, and filled her with my scarlet love.

Someone rushed into the room. "Trudy, are you out of your goddamn mind? Get the fuck away from her!"

While Michelle checked on Ms. Dahl, who'd hit her head on the edge of the bed frame, Bethany ran to the unconscious Mrs. Jones.

Little ol' me?

I escaped to the elevator.

CHAPTER 10
ALEX

"What's going on?" I asked, my breath coming in short gasps after a terrified sprint down the hallway.

Bethany looked at Michelle.

Michelle looked at Bethany.

"I honestly don't know," Bethany finally said, shrugging her shoulders.

"Something super-duper fucked up," Michelle added.

Hearing the yells, the ladies' assigned nurses showed up and, after being told what happened, took over their care. I wasn't keen on them hearing our conversation. "Why don't we take this discussion elsewhere?"

"Sure. Yeah." Bethany seemed dazed by what she'd witnessed.

Alone in the staff lounge, Michelle sat beside Bethany on the sofa, while I poured three cups of coffee. It smelled burnt and unappetizing, but we all desperately needed the caffeine. I suspected it was just the beginning of a very long evening.

"So, you found Trudy?"

"Did we ever!" Michelle said. "Blood covered, naked as the day she was born, and regurgitating on poor old Mrs. Jones."

"Wait...she puked on her?"

"That's the part that stands out to you?" Michelle laughed.

Ignoring Michelle, Bethany leaned forward, voice urgent. "Yes, she puked on her. Why?"

"Delgado vomited on Trudy, and now Trudy has retched on another patient. Don't you find that curious? And why the hell wasn't she wearing clothes?"

"Ah! There it is!" Michelle gave me a high-five, and I chuckled. Her intrinsic playfulness amused me. "Seriously though," she continued, "could it be a contagion? Maybe something that caused hyperpyrexia delirium?"

"Possibly, but if it *is* contagious and the incubation is *that* fast, we need to notify the local health department and the CDC. This floor needs to be locked down, and fast," Bethany said.

"Let's slow our roll and not jump to the worst-case scenario." Michelle patted her hand reassuringly.

"Did either of you see where Trudy went?" I asked.

"I didn't," Michelle said.

Bethany shook her head. "My focus was on the injured patients."

"Damn." I paced back and forth across the room. "So, we don't know for sure she's even still on this floor."

"True that," Michelle said. "But she *does* look like the stripper version of *Carrie* at the prom...so, there's that. She'll be kinda hard to miss."

I stopped pacing and looked at them. "Are we all in agreement that something very strange is happening here, and that Dr. Delgado, who was recently in the Amazonian jungle, is very likely 'patient zero'?"

"Based on the limited information we have right now, yes, I'd say that theory is fair," Bethany said.

Michelle shook her head. "I don't think we should jump to conclusions. It could just be the motherfuckin' king of gastrointestinal inflammation. Nothing more than a hardcore stomach bug."

"You're not wrong," Bethany said, trying hard to be diplomatic.

"But there are things you don't know. And...there's something else that's been bothering me."

"What's that?" I asked.

"When we saw Trudy, she was wearing this big, crazed grin...like Delgado's. It scared me, honestly. She looked, well...she looked mentally unstable. Also, I don't know if Michelle noticed this or not, but Trudy completely ignored Ms. Dahl, shoving her out of the way, and went straight for poor Mrs. Jones like she had an agenda. Why one and not the other?"

"Oh, yeah," said Michelle. "I did notice that. Ms. Dahl walked right up to Trudy. She would have been an easy target, but Trudy beelined for sweet little Marge instead."

"So, what are you saying?" I wasn't sure where they were going with this.

"Well, it, uh, kinda seemed like she knew who she wanted...like maybe she'd already picked Mrs. Jones out," Bethany responded.

"Maybe there was bad blood between them?" I suggested. "Maybe it was personal?"

"Not a chance," Michelle said. "Trudy wouldn't have bad blood with anyone. She's the nicest, most accommodating nursing assistant I've worked with. The patients adore her."

"So, why would she have gone specifically for Mrs. Jones?"

Silence. The air was thick with notes of anxiety and fear.

Bethany cleared her throat. "It almost seemed like...like she was going for the weaker prey."

CHAPTER 11

BETHANY

I was immediately embarrassed by my ridiculous statement, yet...it felt right. In my gut, I knew I was on the right track. Something was very wrong inside the walls of this hospital, and I was determined to figure it out and fix it.

"Maybe we should check Delgado's body," I said. "See if it'll give up any secrets."

"Good idea," Alex said. "Let's garb up. Until we have some answers, I'm not taking any chances."

I took a sip of the coffee, grimaced, remembered I'd called it ass sludge earlier, and set the cup on the table. My heart thumped erratically inside my chest as I donned the protective clothing. Hurrying out of the lounge, I felt Michelle place her hand on the small of my back. It was warm, comforting. I liked it.

My gait slowed as we neared the room at the end of the hallway. I could lie to myself all day, but the truth was, all this—everything that had happened so far—was genuinely scary.

Turns out, the foreboding was real.

Alex went inside. Michelle followed. I stood in the hallway gathering my courage.

"What is *happening* around here?" Alex yelled, sounding pissed. My curiosity got the better of me, and I ran into the room.

"I take it this isn't how you left him?" Michelle asked.

"No. It most certainly is not. Someone messed with him. We got him cleaned up, placed him inside the bag, and zipped it up tight. The plan was to take him to the morgue as soon as the paperwork was complete, but things have since gone a little sideways."

The body bag was wide open, Delgado's body covered in smears of dried *human* blood. Blue puddles had formed on the white-tiled floor surrounding his bed. His penis was erect, which wasn't such a big deal. Rigor mortis could cause that. But...

"Is that...semen?" I could hear my voice getting higher pitched with each syllable.

"What?" Alex glanced at Delgado's genitalia, unable to hide his surprise. "Nah...surely not."

"You're obsessed with semen, girl," Michelle said, amused. She leaned closer to the body than I would have, pulled the mask off her nose, and gave it a sniff. "Yep. Smells like the good doctor recently splooged."

I groaned. "Jesus, Michelle, that's gross! He's dead!"

"I call 'em like I see 'em."

"Or smell 'em." Alex pulled some forceps from his pocket and plucked a translucent flake off the corpse's shaft. "I think Michelle is right. This looks a lot like dried vaginal secretion."

"Oh my God." I fell into the visitor's chair beside the bed, knees weak, stomach churning. "Now you're telling me we have a necrophile on the floor? What next? Cannibals?"

"But how did *he* ejaculate? He's a cadaver! A stiff! A carcass!" Even Michelle was riled.

"Well, theoretically, it's possible, I suppose. Rigor in the scrotum's dartos muscle can lead to post-mortem ejaculation," Alex explained. "It tends to happen more to those who were hanged, but it's still physiologically feasible."

"Did Trudy do this?" Michelle asked.

"That's my best guess," Alex answered. "He got red on him some-how, and I haven't seen any other blood-covered streakers. Have you?"

Michelle casually popped a mint into her mouth. "So, we have a necrophile streaker, who used to be one of our most valued employ-ees, vomiting blood on patients' faces? Sounds legit."

"Guys..." I said.

"That's about it, yes." Alex went to the sink and rinsed off his forceps.

"Guys, I think you need to..."

"It sounds like a shitty, low-budget horror film."

"GUYS!" I shouted.

Any other time, their identical shocked expressions would have been humorous. Not now.

"Look at Delgado!" I said sharply.

Three sets of eyes gazed at the rippling and undulating, the bulging and deflating, of Delgado's skin.

"I knew there was something inside him!" I said, backing away from the bed. "I fucking knew it!"

"What...the hell...is happening?" Michelle asked, voice tense.

"Bethany and I have both witnessed some impossibilities with this body today. Now you're getting a taste, too."

"Okay. We should probably call Dr. Reznik." Michelle said, peering at the body. For the first time, she looked frightened.

Alex glanced at me. "What do you think? Should we fill Reznik in?"

"It couldn't hurt. We're in over our heads. Maybe she can help."

"All right. I'll page her. You and Michelle do a quick scan of the patients' rooms...see if you can find Trudy. I'm sure the doc will want to see her too. Just...make sure to close the door behind you when you leave this room."

"Good call," Michelle said, grabbing the handle and pulling it firmly shut.

We marched down the hallway, determined to make things right.

Multiple call lights began alarming.

CHAPTER 12
DEE

This fucking job...I hated every minute I was here. I could be home, performing on OnlyFans, letting guys gaze at my body, hearing their compliments, feeling like a princess, accepting their expensive gifts, reveling in the way they *wanted me*. Instead, I was in this shit-smelling, germ infested crypt. Worse, after dealing with managerial bullshit and inept staff all day, I had a pounding headache that just wouldn't quit.

No one appreciates me.

I'd always been positive. Happy. Upbeat. I was fair to the other nurses. Hell, ask anyone...I was a model charge nurse. But did I get any love? Not a single goddamn bit. I mean, I certainly couldn't help that I was promoted to charge nurse because I was the best for the job. I knew Bethany was jealous, but Bethany had *always* been jealous of me. Poor girl nearly flunked out of college—and would have!—if not for my endless help and guidance. She should've worshiped the very ground I walked on. Instead, she mocked me... thought I didn't see her rolling her eyes behind my back.

Well, fuck her! Fuck them all! As soon as I've built up my fan base,

I'll be quitting this lame-ass job and living off my on-line income! I deserve that and so much more!

Patient call lights started alarming.

They didn't stop.

Lazy little pissants! I'll be calling a staff meeting first thing Monday morning and putting these goddamn nurses in their place!

I angrily threw open the door to my office. It hit against the wall with a loud bang and swung back around, bonking me on the back of the head.

"Fuck!" I shrieked, rubbing the tender flesh. My headache was now ten times worse.

Not a soul lingered in the hallway, but there *was* blood. Lots of it.

That's it! Someone is getting fired!

If another charge nurse saw this mess, they'd report it, just to bring me down. *What had I done to make everyone in this medical center is so damn jealous of me?*

I found Michelle, Alex, and my doormat college roommate, Bethany, hovering in the hallway just around the corner.

"Alex, what the hell are you still doing here? Get back to the ER now, or I'll call your superior. Michelle, find some help and answer the damn call lights. Bethany, get the mop bucket and clean up this disgusting mess."

They did nothing. Simply gaped like the fucking idiots they were.

"The shit you waiting for? I gave you all orders, and I expect you to do them. I don't mean ten minutes from now, I mean stat!"

I turned and stomped back to my office, once again slamming the door closed.

What would these idiots do without me?

CHAPTER 13
MICHELLE

"A narcissist on a power trip. Woohoo!" I said, peppy jazz hands showing my enthusiasm. "Listen, I'm going to go check the patients as our dear charge nurse requested. These call light alarms are driving me batshit. You guys proceed with your original tasks. Dee will never know. She won't leave her office until it's time to go home."

"Fine by me," Alex said, heading to the front desk to page Dr. Reznik. "She's not my charge."

I stopped Bethany as she walked away. "Hey!"

She turned. "Yes?"

"Be careful, okay?"

She smiled. "Of course. Back atcha."

Entering the first room, I turned off the call light using the wall switch, then faced the two beds.

"What can I do for you, Mr. Olsen?"

"I think something's wrong with Mr. Schmidt. His curtain is closed, and he won't answer me. I keep hearing gagging sounds."

I smiled reassuringly. "I'll check it out. Don't you worry, okay?"

Walking across the room to Mr. Schmidt's bed, I already dreaded what I was about to find. Bracing myself for the worst-case scenario, I yanked the curtain aside...and screamed. A fountain of blood cascaded from his throat, gracefully arcing into the air before splattering across his withered face.

For the first time in my nursing career, I felt helpless to assist a patient. Poor Mr. Schmidt was a lost cause. There was nothing I could do. He'd lost *a lot* of blood.

But I could save Mr. Olsen. Assisting the elderly man—whose broken hip prevented him from walking—into the wheelchair, I rushed to the staff lounge. Once there, I grabbed a bottle of Lysol from the counter, the only reasonable weapon I could find, and handed it to him. "Anyone tries to bother you, do not hesitate to spray this in their face, okay?"

"Am I in danger, miss?

I started to reassure him, then shrugged instead. "You know what? I really don't know. What I can tell you with absolute certainty is that I'll do everything I can to keep you and the others safe. Do you believe that?"

His voice was fragile. "Y-y-y-es."

"Good. Help yourself to anything in the fridge and be strong. I'll be back as soon as I can."

He said nothing, just solemnly nodded.

I went to the next room.

What I saw there was even worse.

CHAPTER 14

BETHANY

I had no luck finding Trudy. It scared me to think she was roaming free and wreaking havoc throughout the hospital, but it would have been easy to slip away during the commotion. And what was wrong with her? Did she need help too? I felt sick. Trudy was my friend.

Ahead, I watched Dr. Reznik and Alex enter Delgado's room. I joined them, hoping to see Michelle. She wasn't there.

Dr. Reznik stared at the twitching corpse with morbid fascination. When she spoke, her voice was distant...almost *dreamy*. "Alex, fetch me a chest tube insertion kit, will ya? I need the scalpel from inside."

"Why do you need a scalpel?" I asked.

"I intend to cut this man open."

I gaped, then choked on my own saliva. That was not the answer I expected. Alex returned with the kit, seemingly on board with her plan. Still coughing, I asked, "Can you *do* that?"

"Probably not. I'm not a forensic pathologist or medical examiner, but given the situation we find ourselves in, I think it's entirely appropriate. We need information, and we need it now. Don't you agree?"

"I guess I do." Clearing my throat, I said, "But what about his family?"

"His contact person couldn't even be bothered to talk to me when I called. If his family has a problem with it, they can take it up with me." She pulled the scalpel from the kit, just as Michelle entered the room. I'd never been so grateful to see anyone in my life, despite her wan, pale appearance.

"You okay?" I mouthed. Instead of answering, she gave me a weak thumbs up, but the look in her eyes was anything but. They appeared haunted.

Once we were all decked out in our protective gear, Dr. Reznik said, "I'm going to make a midline incision, starting at the xiphoid process, passing around the umbilicus, and stopping at the pubis symphysis. That should give me total access to everything in his abdominal cavity."

I wasn't sure why she was sharing that information. One didn't get through nursing school without learning all about midline incisions. I suspected she was nervous, and this was a calming tactic.

I felt for her.

Taking a deep breath, Dr. Reznik placed the scalpel against Delgado's mottled skin and made the first incision. As she slowly made her way through the various layers of tissue—and a great deal of adipose—the tension grew.

"All right, here we go," she said several minutes later, slicing through the final layer. She didn't have any retractors—we weren't in the operating room—so she very carefully used her hands to pull apart the two sides. What she saw inside the body caused her breathing to become so erratic, I worried she might pass out.

"What is it?" Alex asked, trying to peer over her shoulder.

When she was finally able to speak, her voice was haggard. "Have a look for yourselves." As she stepped away from Delgado's remains, we moved tentatively forward, peering into his gaping core.

Alex recoiled. "Jesus! What is it? Organ stew?"

"Essentially, yeah. They've...liquefied."

"Could it be post-mortem decay?" Michelle asked.

Dr. Reznik laughed briefly. "In a couple hours? No."

"Then...what?" I asked, grabbing the extra-long forceps from the kit. "And what the hell is this?" Dipping the metal tongs into the visceral goo, I pulled out a large clump of...something.

"Put it in here," Dr. Reznik instructed, handing me an emesis basin.

I obliged, my hands shaking. It appeared to be thousands of threads woven tightly together. Alex took the forceps from me and gently worked them apart. With the stained exterior removed, the interior was silky white.

"It's sticky," Alex said, as he worked to separate the strands.

"Oh my God!" Michelle blurted. "That's spider webbing!"

"Be careful around it! That stuff has some sort of acidic coating on it!" Alex cautioned.

Despite everything, spider webbing inside a human body was so far out of the realm of possibility, I felt myself firmly denying what I was seeing. "That seems...unlikely."

"No, I think she's right," said Alex. "We knew something was inside him. Hell, after I saw that hairy leg poking out of his ear, a part of me kept thinking *tarantula*. But it's such a ridiculous theory, I never *really* let myself go there."

"How can a spider...tarantula...*whatever*...how can it even survive inside a human body?" asked Michelle.

I composed myself, compartmentalizing my doubts, and rattled off some facts. "Tarantulas use their fangs to immobilize their prey, then inject them with digestive enzymes, which liquefies flesh and organs. They have tube-like appendages beneath their fangs called pedipalps that allow them to suck the liquid into their stomachs. Clearly, it was feeding on Delgado. They do need oxygen, though, so I'm not sure how it managed to breathe." The astonished looks on my peers' faces forced me to add, "I used to raise tarantulas when I was in high school. I know a bit about them."

"That's useful information. Thank you." Dr. Reznik cleared her throat. "But it still doesn't explain how a tarantula ended up in Delgado's body...or how it survived in such an environment."

The silence grew heavy as we stared into the muck that had once been Francisco Delgado.

"I think something about its venom has anticoagulant properties. It's the only thing that would explain all the hemorrhaging and blood today," Alex said.

Needing to get it off her chest, Michelle blurted, "Trudy vomited blood on at least six patients, probably more. That's why so many call lights were going off. Most of the recipients were in rough shape. Their roommates were understandably freaked out, so I moved them to the staff lounge...just in case."

"Jesus," Alex muttered.

"Well, that's heartbreaking. Are we going to lose the patients she puked on?" I said, now even more worried. Fucking Dee should be dealing with all this. She could Snapchat with her boy toys on her own time.

"You saw what happened with Delgado, Bethany," Alex said. "There was nothing we could do. He was doomed from the moment he encountered...whatever it was he encountered...in the jungle."

Dr. Reznik paced around the room. "What does it all mean? For the life of me, I can't get the pieces to fit."

"To add another layer of craziness, when we coded him, white threads floated around the body. It's what caused the gash on the back of my hand," Alex said, showing off the bandage I'd applied earlier.

"Yeah, the webbing got Trudy too," I said. "She had a nasty looking wound on her arm I never got the chance to clean and dress."

"How could webbing cause injuries? It's just silk! And how did I miss seeing them?" Dr. Reznik asked incredulously.

Alex looked her in the eye. "I can't answer either of those questions, doc. All I can say with any certainty is the webbing is coated in some substance that easily dissolves human flesh. It's safe to say we're dealing with a very dangerous arachnid. Maybe even something the world has never seen."

Dr. Reznik's glanced at the corpse. "But...where is it?"

CHAPTER 15

DEE

At least the fucking alarms stopped.

As I put the final touches on a message to my boyfriend, Chad, I decided he might like a racy little photo. I locked my office door and snapped a few shots. Chad was going to be a very happy boy when he saw the way I was sprawled across my desk wearing nothing but an old-fashioned nurse's cap and stethoscope.

After redressing and answering a quick call from my other boyfriend, Matt, I sent him a photo too, then figured it was time to head home. The bitchy overlords only allowed so much unapproved overtime.

For months, I'd been trying to figure out a way to get Bethany fired...or at least transferred. I was sick of seeing her dopey face everywhere, and I knew she was turning the rest of the staff against me. Why else would they hate me so much? But today's shift had been a goldmine of disasters. I'd simply lay the blame at her feet when I talked to the nurse manager.

Satisfied with life, I pushed 'send' on Chad's message and packed my tote bag.

Something *large* scurried across the wall. I jumped and let out an undignified screech.

But...it was gone.

I hmphed and straightened my clothes. Hopefully nobody heard. I was stressed, overtired, and needed my hot tub. As I shut down the computer, my private cell rang again. This time it was Chad.

"Hey, baby!" I answered in my most feminine, seductive voice. "Ooh, you liked that picture? I'm so glad. I took it just for you."

Five minutes later, still talking to Chad, something thumped behind me.

I looked, saw nothing, and continued regaling Chad with my latest masturbatory tale.

Another thump.

"Chad, can you hold on for a second, baby? I need to check something." I listened to his response. "Of course! I'll be right back. Promise you'll stay hard for me!"

Placing the cell on my desk, I went to the filing cabinets, which is wear the noise seemed to be originating from. Examining the metal exteriors, I found nothing, so I pulled open the drawers. Zilch. Just folder after folder of bullshit paperwork and employee files. Annoyed, knowing I hadn't imagined the noises, I opened the final drawer.

"The fuck?"

Lace-like white threads covered the contents. A little spider had made himself a cozy home in my file cabinet...but it was soon to be evicted. Not wanting to touch the creature, or its nasty web, I put on a latex glove.

"Come on, little buddy," I said, pushing the webbing out of the way. "Time for you to meet the tread on my shoe."

I felt something touch my finger. I couldn't see it, but I smiled, knowing I was seconds away from some well-deserved physical violence.

"Well, hello there. Nice meeting you too. Why not come out and meet your fate, my eight-legged pal?"

I could no longer feel it. Seconds passed. Nothing happened. "Okay, you little fucker, you're boring me, and I don't like being bored."

Something wrapped around my hand, encasing it completely.

But...that can't be right...

It squeezed, crushing bones. Tears filled my eyes, and another pained shriek erupted. This time, I didn't care who heard.

Yanking my hand from the drawer, I finally saw my nemesis. Eight circular, black soulless eyes. Eight legs, covered in coarse, metallic purple hair. Two huge fangs. A scream built inside my throat, but only a whimper escaped as the muscles in my throat seized in fear. I could hear Chad repeatedly yelling my name through the phone, but I was frozen...immobile.

Why was a tarantula living in Duluth?

The dinner-plate sized spider walked slowly up my arm. Its hairs tickled my skin as it inched closer and closer to my face. Paralysis finally ebbing, I backed slowly toward the door, not wanting to aggravate the monster hovering on my shoulder. I knew if I tried to knock it off, it would come back immediately...bigger, meaner. I turned the knob with my uninjured hand...nothing happened.

Shit! I didn't unlock it after my photo shoot!

As I fumbled with the lock, the tarantula wrapped around my face, the claws on its feet burying into my skin. The door wouldn't budge, so I did the only thing I could...I screamed.

"Help! Help me!"

Chad's tinny voice was frantic through the phone's speakers.

Flashes of light consumed my vision as a needle-like appendage plunged into my right eye. The burning was so brutal, it was indescribable. A gelatinous liquid flowed down my cheek just before an intense pressure filled the socket. That was followed by thunderous sucking sounds and a disquieting emptying. Tears poured from both ducts. I knew if this abomination were to lose interest, I'd be left a blind, eyeless freak...which, I supposed, was better than the alternative.

The tarantula reared back, a bristly leg carefully assessing my orbital socket. Finding the sweet spot, it pushed. I could feel bone splintering and widening as I fell to the floor. The last thing I heard before the fanged obscenity shoved its way into my brain was Chad...

"Dee, you can't just leave a guy hanging. What the hell do you expect me to do with this stiffy?"

CHAPTER 16

BETHANY

I'd just wanted a simple night at home...good food, good movies, a phone call from a beautiful nurse. Instead, I was stuck in a hospital where things were going to hell quicker than I could say, "Boo!" The one saving grace: I was sitting beside Michelle, and she was holding my shaking hand.

"I brought in two of my colleagues so we could discuss this situation and strategize," Dr. Reznik said, giving each of us an encouraging smile. "I need to tell you, though...things are worse than we initially thought. *Much* worse. The virus—or whatever it is we're dealing with—has spread to various floors in the hospital, yet no one has seen Trudy. How we keep missing a bloody, naked women roaming the halls, I'm not sure. Strange, indeed. But the bigger concern is that I notified the local health department and CDC offices. Both were already aware of the situation, though they refused to share how they knew."

"Do you think one of the other physicians notified them?" I asked.

"Possibly." She paused, staring at her shoes. "Look, I don't really know how to say this, but seeing is believing. Peek outside." None of us moved. "Go on. You need to see what's happening."

We walked to the floor-to-ceiling windows near the elevator. Helicopters flew overhead. Four floors down, emergency vehicles were parked haphazardly, their lights flashing a multitude of hues. People dressed in head-to-toe personal protective equipment, including respirator masks, ran frantically around the parking lot. The National Guard had been deployed, and each soldier carried an automatic assault rifle. A half-mile out, near the perimeter, news vans with four-letter call signs painted on the side sat quietly as their on-scene reporters broadcast the breaking news.

"May God save us all," Alex mumbled.

"We're so fucked," said Michelle.

"I'm scared," I whispered. Michelle heard and gave me a hug.

Dr. Reznik, looking tired, said, "Did any of you even notice the next shift of nurses never showed up?"

I glanced at my watch, eyes widening. My shift had ended ninety minutes ago. "I've been so busy and distracted, I hadn't noticed the time. Will they not let the night shift staff in? How long have we been quarantined?"

"I'm not sure, but it doesn't matter," Dr. Reznik said. "We're stuck here, and we're the first line of defense for all these patients. I suggest we get the fourth floor squared away...meet everyone's needs, give them any meds that are due, and make them as safe and comfortable as possible. Then we should figure this shit out and worry about saving ourselves."

We raided the snack fridge and took the patients in the staff lounge some Jell-O, crackers, ginger ale, and a few questionable looking peanut butter and jelly sandwiches. They were scared and exhausted, so we supplied them with pillows and blankets from the laundry cart, and a few cots I found in the supply closet.

"Unfortunately, the staff bathroom is off limits. It's a biohazard area, so avoid it at all costs. There is a public bathroom directly across the hall, so if you need to go, use that. Just please, and I can't stress this enough, be careful. By now, you've seen and heard enough to know we're dealing with something very bad. Take heed," Michelle lectured.

Between the six of us—Michelle, Alex, myself, and the three doctors—we visited each patient room, provided folks with basic necessities, and did our best to explain the situation without frightening them. Immobile patients were moved into rooms with those who were ambulatory, and we suggested they barricade their doors after we left. For those visited by Trudy, we simply closed their doors, tying the door handle and anchoring it to whatever hefty items we could find on the ward. This was an unprecedented situation. We did the best we could, playing everything by ear and hoping for the best.

"Why isn't my cell working?" a patient asked.

"Hm. I'm not sure. Mine was working fine a few minutes ago. Let me check." Sure enough, I had no service either. "Seems our connection is down." I smiled reassuringly. "I'm sure it will be up again in no time. Why don't you watch some television?"

I found a fun, romantic comedy and left as quickly as I could.

"I think they've blocked our cell reception...nothing works. As far as I can tell, we can't even make calls," I told Michelle and Alex. They pulled out their phones.

"Well, shit," Michelle said, staring at her screen.

Alex looked worried as he tucked his back into his pocket. "That can't be good."

"No," I said, watching several of the ward's nurses get on the elevator and descend to the lobby.

When the floor was finally secured, we gathered again at the nurse's station.

"Okay, let's brainstorm," Dr. Reznik said.

"Shouldn't we get Dee?" Michelle asked.

"Yeah, let's willingly make the situation worse," I grumbled. Alex chuckled, but Michelle was disapproving.

"She's the charge nurse, Bethany. She needs to be in on this."

"Exactly. I couldn't agree more. But what has she done so far?

She should have been out here helping us the entire time, not having phone sex in her office."

Michelle looked at me curiously. "Okay. Interesting point, but I'm still going to get her." She walked down the short hall to the charge nurse's office. I waited to hear her knock. Instead, there was a long pause followed by, "Uh, you guys might want to see this."

Already filled with uncontrollable dread, I ran to her side. Rust-colored blood seeped from the crack beneath the door.

"Oh God! We need to get in there." Dr. Reznik pounded on the door, simultaneously turning the handle...to no avail. "Why is it locked?"

"Because she spends most of her workday chatting with guys on social media," I said, tired of covering for the one person who treated me like dog shit.

"I bet there's a key in the nurse manager's office," Michelle said, hurrying to the office to check.

"Dee, are you okay in there?" Dr. Reznik called out. "We're here to help."

A gentle thump was the only response.

Hearing the sound, Dr. Reznik forcefully plowed against the door with her shoulder, attempting to break in. "She may not have much time. We need to get to her!"

"I have the key!" Michelle said, sprinting toward them. She inserted it inside the lock, turned the handle, and swung open the door.

Dee faced away from us, standing in the corner. Her body spasmodically twitched and jerked, the movements reminding me of an end-stage Huntington's disease patient I'd once cared for. She looked...wrong. Joints bending in unnatural directions, muscles straining, ligaments popping.

I stepped forward. After living with her for two years, I still felt oddly responsible for this despicable human being. "Dee, are you okay? Why don't you let us help—"

She gracelessly turned, dropping her cell phone on the floor. The screen shattered. Through the cracks, it appeared she'd been trying to take a *selfie*.

Yep. That tracked.

I heard Dr. Reznik gasp. That's when I finally noticed the state of Dee's head. Or what remained of it. Recoiling and stumbling backward, I couldn't take my eyes off the obscenity she'd become.

Her eyeball was gone. The socket was split apart, and liquefied brain matter leaked from the fracture. The same blue fluid we'd seen oozing from Delgado trailed down Dee's cheeks. Long, purple hairs grew from her nostrils. With the structural integrity of her skull compromised, the rest of her face had caved in, the skull cleaved in two. The spider leg protruding from the top of her head and the demented smile painted across her face—made far worse by the inhuman appearance of her body—created the vilest horror movie monster I'd ever seen.

I screamed and ran from the room, triggering her predatory instincts. She hissed and ran after me, but before she could reach the door with her stilted gate, Alex slammed it shut, and Michelle reengaged the lock.

"We're going to die! We're all going to die!" Thoroughly frightened, I couldn't stop the pessimistic, panic-induced mantra.

Dr. Reznik slapped me. "Get it together! We don't have time for this. If we're going to survive the night, we need you with us. Take some deep breaths and calm down."

Michelle, eyes troubled but still grinning, said, "Look on the bright side, Bethany...no more shifts with Dee."

CHAPTER 17

ALEX

"What's our next move?" I looked at the small group of misfits surrounding me, knowing our lives would never be the same after tonight.

Dr. Starkweather, an orthopedic surgeon and a dead ringer for Santa Claus, spoke up. "I'll tell you *my* next move. It's my twentieth wedding anniversary, and I have plans with my beautiful wife. I've been here almost eighteen hours, and they can't make me stay. We have rights."

"I don't think that's a great idea, Daniel. They have guns," Dr. Reznik said. "Please reconsider. Your wife would prefer you stay safe."

"I'll be fine. And I'm not so sure I'm safe here, sorry to say. I mean, that poor nurse," he said, gesturing to Dee's office. "Besides, they're not going to shoot before they hear what I have to say. I promise I won't take any unnecessary risks." He stood. "I'd love for all of you to come with me." When nobody moved, he nodded and offered an understanding smile. "Best of luck to you then. I'll do what I can from the outside."

Dr. Reznik looked sad as the elevator door slid shut behind him.

"Well, that's unfortunate, but I don't have the luxury of worrying about him right now. We need to figure out where they're headed and what their plan is."

"Who is 'they?'" asked Dr. Cherikoff.

Dr. Reznik exhaled loudly and shrugged. "The...spiders? Their human puppets? Fuck if I know."

"What do we know, high-level? Let's put it all on the table," Michelle said.

"We know Delgado specialized in arachnids, worked for a research facility here in Duluth, and was in the Amazonian jungle for weeks," I began. "He arrived home yesterday and ended up in the hospital today with severe vomiting and bleeding. Negative for all the scary viral shit. Diagnosed with acute hemorrhagic gastroenteritis and admitted to the fourth floor, where he went downhill quickly. Bethany and I both witnessed something moving inside him as his mental status deteriorated. He vomited a mixture of blood and bile onto a CNA named Trudy, who did the same thing to several other patients and then seemingly disappeared. We locked the patients Trudy attacked in their rooms, as a precautionary measure."

"Has anyone checked on them recently?" Bethany asked. "None of this is their fault. They still deserve our care."

"No, and we should leave them be. They're dangerous. Our focus must shift to those we can save." Michelle shrugged and looked at Bethany apologetically.

"Are we good with that? Bethany?" I asked. "For the record, I agree with Michelle."

"As do we," Dr. Reznik said. Dr. Cherikoff gave a brief nod.

"It just feels wrong." Bethany answered, deflated. "But I can see it's the right choice."

"So we're all on the same page. Excellent." I continued plying everyone with information. "Delgado died, and you, Dr. Reznik, dissected him, only to find his organs liquefied and wrapped in what appeared to be spider webbing. Yet, we could find no spider. There were white globules in that bathroom mess. Could those be spider eggs?" I shrugged. "Maybe. Maybe not. It's plausible, but your guess is as good as mine. Then we discovered Dee with a missing eyeball and a spider leg protruding from her head. She tried to attack Bethany. And that's my spiel."

Dr. Reznik added, "We also know the contamination is spreading throughout the hospital at a rapid rate, and somehow, the powers-that-be already knew. We know the hospital is locked down, and, from what I'm seeing outside, it's a safe bet we won't be allowed to leave. I suspect we're here for the duration."

Bethany raised her hand. "May I say something?"

I smiled at her schoolgirl innocence. "Of course."

"I've been thinking about this a lot." She pushed some loose wisps of hair behind her ears. "When we saw Trudy attack those two women, she went straight for the weaker of the two. Do you think it's possible that, since these tarantulas are almost certainly parasitic, compromised immune systems make bodies easier to take over and control? If there isn't much of an immune system to mount an adaptive response, the spider can take over its host and control it that much easier."

Silence reigned.

"As much as I hate pondering such an awful theory, I think you're on to something," Michelle finally said. "It makes sense."

"It does." I smiled at Bethany, silently thanking her for such valuable insight. "And if you remember, the eosinophil levels in Delgado's ER blood work were through the roof. That can be indicative of parasites. Right, Doc?" I directed the question at Reznik, but Cherikoff, the infectious disease physician, responded.

"That's correct. We see it frequently when patients have traveled to third-world countries and come home full of parasitic worms. I imagine lab results would be similar for a parasitic spider."

"So, are we surmising that Delgado acquired some sort of freakish arachnid monstrosity during his trip to Peru, which remained dormant until he arrived back in the states?" I asked.

"It's possible," Cherikoff said, stroking his beard. "Parasites can go dormant for extended periods of time. That's why we often don't see them in stool samples, even though they're clearly infecting the host. They're not necessarily dormant, but their life cycles are such that they're inactive for periods of time. Perhaps that's what happened here."

"Then why is everything happening so fast now?" Bethany's acute panic attack had subsided, but it was obvious by the shrill voice that her anxiety was still high.

"You've already answered your own question, Bethany. Patients sick enough to be admitted to hospitals, *especially* these days with insurance companies fighting us every step of the way, are likely to have poorly functioning immune systems. When there is no fight from the host, things can progress more quickly for the parasite."

Bethany's nose crinkled in concentration as she considered her next question. "Okay, so based on this theory, where would the spiders go next?"

"Seems pretty obvious to me," Cherikoff responded.

"Where?" I asked.

Cherikoff took his time answering. "I suspect they're heading to the children's cancer ward...if they're not already there."

CHAPTER 18

DR. DANIEL STARKWEATHER

I wasn't as confident as I'd led the others to believe. My knees were shaking like they did the day I took the MCAT exam, and I was sweating like Robert Hays in *Airplane!* I chuckled thinking about that scene, then sobered just as quickly. Those dudes outside had big guns, and the way they were strutting around, they weren't afraid to use them.

Still...Lena was at home waiting for me. Our fancy restaurant reservation had long since passed, but that didn't matter. If all else failed, I knew she'd be perfectly happy going to Applebee's, the site of our very first date. She wanted only to spend time with me, never caring where we went, as long as we were together. I was a very lucky man.

She'd taken the kids to their grandparents' house for the night, so they weren't home right now to help distract her from worrying about me. I smiled thinking about our babies. I'd become a dad late in life—Lena was almost fifteen years my junior—which made me appreciate them more. Ruby looked just like me (before I'd turned into jolly old St. Nick), while Phillip favored his mom. It was a source of amusement for us throughout the years, though Lena swore they both acted just like me.

With the phones knocked out, I couldn't even call her. I knew she must be frantic, and I simply couldn't bear the thought of her being lonely and afraid on our anniversary.

Your worry is nearly over, sweetheart. I'm on my way.

The elevator arrived at the ground floor, doors opening to utter chaos. People—some blood-covered, some not—were crying, screaming, making threats. Some were lying on the floor. I couldn't tell if they were alive or dead. Others were twitching and jerking...just like Dee. I rushed past the crowds and headed to the revolving front doors.

"I wouldn't do that, if'n I was you."

I looked at a man sitting in his chair, smoking a cigarette, and calmly watching the mayhem surrounding him.

Maybe he knew something I didn't. "Oh yeah? Why's that? I'm a surgeon here, not a patient."

"Ya think that's gonna save ya?" He threw back his head and laughed. "Listen, Mr. Surgeon...this here hospital has been kwoor-oh-teened. Them out there is some cold-blooded soldiers, and they'd just as soon kill you as not. Don't matter whether youz a fancy doctor. That don't mean squat to them. Their orders is to contain whatever's happenin' in here. You mark my words."

I could see something moving inside his neck; something just below the skin. I needed to go. Get away. Escape now. "Thank you for your wisdom and advice, sir, but I'll be fine." I pushed through the rotating doors and came face to face with the muzzle of a gun.

"STOP RIGHT THERE! GET BACK INSIDE! THIS IS YOUR FIRST AND ONLY WARNING!"

I raised my hands in the air to show I was unarmed. "Thank you for your concern and for the excellent job you're doing protecting everyone. My name is Dan Starkweather. I'm an orthopedic surgeon. I'm perfectly fine...no cooties here. I just want to get home to my wife. It's our anniv—"

Gunshots rang out. I could feel sharp punches all over my body. They took my breath away, but there was no pain. Just surreal disbelief that I was living my final moments.

I sat down hard on the blacktop.

Lena will understand and appreciate what I tried to do for her. I hope she finds somebody who makes her as happy as she makes me.

A shot to my left shoulder knocked me backward.

Ruby and Phillip won't have a daddy anymore. They'll have to visit my grave. I hope they'll remember how much I love them.

A soldier stood above me, his rifle pointed at my forehead. From inside, I could hear the man who had warned me laughing.

I just wanted to get home to my family. That's all. Just go home to my fam—

CHAPTER 19

DR. REZNIK

"How did I not consider the children?" I felt sick to my stomach. "We need to gather whatever weapons we can find and head up there! I will not have innocent babies dying on my watch."

"Sure would be nice to have a gun," Michelle said.

Dr. Cherikoff snorted. "Well, we sure aren't finding one of those in this hospital."

The distant staccato tapping of an automatic rifle caught our attention.

"Fuck!" I shouted, rushing toward the window. Seconds later, the others joined me...but not before I'd cried out in shocked horror. Seventy-five feet below, dark blood puddling beneath his prone body, was Dan Starkweather. Bullet holes riddled his frame from head to toe.

"I can't believe those fuckers shot him! There must be twenty wounds! What the hell?" Dr. Cherikoff asked, shock evident in his voice.

"I know Dan quite well. He was nothing but calm and reasonable. Shooting him means they'll shoot any of us. They're killing

79

without discretion, which means they're petrified." I paused and then, voice flat and robotic, "They're never letting us out of here."

Alex placed his forehead against the cool glass, struggling to breathe, and closing his eyes against the horror below.

Bethany sniffled, wiping away tears.

"Happy anniversary, Dan's wife," Michelle whispered, fighting back her own salty tears.

CHAPTER 20

BETHANY

"We need weapons. Lots of them," I said, opening cabinets and searching for anything that might help us fight.

"Get all the scalpels out of the chest tube kits," Dr. Reznik said. Grab any spinal needles you can find. They're almost four inches long...that should do some damage. Scissors would be good. If any of you have pepper spray in your handbags, get it. I'm going to load up several syringes with propofol...if all else fails, maybe we can send some folks into the land of unconsciousness." Grabbing several ten milliliter syringes, she filled them with the milky fluid.

"I have pepper spray! I'll get it and check out the rest of the lockers...see if I can find any goodies that aren't locked up," Michelle said.

"Good idea," Dr. Reznik said.

"I'm going to grab a few things from my office," Dr. Cherikoff said. "Only be a minute."

"Sure. No problem." Alex responded, watching him disappear down the hallway. Then, "You know, there might be confiscated guns or knives in the ER. You'd be surprised how many folks bring that shit to the hospital with them."

Dr. Reznik shook her head. "I talked to a colleague just before our phones died. She was hiding in a supply closet. Said the ER was overrun with spiders and hemorrhaging victims. Half the staff is either dead or infected. Those remaining planned to abandon the area and head to a higher, safer floor. They're surely long gone by now. It's not worth going down there, Alex."

"Half the ER staff?" Alex asked, his voice small.

"Yes." She rested a hand on his shoulder. "I know they were your work family. I'm sorry, Alex."

"I'm sorry too, Alex," I said.

He nodded but didn't respond. Discreetly wiping his eyes, he continued searching the sterile kits for weapons.

"Do we have anything heavy we can put inside pillowcases to do some pummeling?" Dr. Reznik asked.

"Hm. Let me think." I rubbed my fingers over my temples trying to stave off a rapidly growing headache. "What about the portable EKG machines? I believe we have three. Those weigh, what? Maybe four pounds each? That would allow us to wallop someone pretty hard. And it's not too heavy to carry for extended periods. Oh! And we need to collect all the fire extinguishers we can find too!"

"Great ideas!" Dr. Reznik said, giving me a quick wink.

"Thanks, Dr. Reznik."

"Please, call me Taytum."

Touched, I said, "Thank you, I will."

"Hey, I found a few cans of pepper spray!" Michelle said, returning from the nurse's lounge.

"How is everyone holding up in there?"

"They're sleeping. Seem fine."

I hoped all our patients were sleeping through this nightmare.

Ten minutes later, we were fully armed. In our pockets, we each had a pair of sharp scissors, a scalpel, a few four-inch needles placed on syringes for easier stabbing, twenty milliliters of propofol divided into two syringes with capped needles, and a can of pepper spray. Everyone but Alex had a pillowcase filled with a portable EKG machine. Since there were only three, Alex's pillowcase contained an unused IV pump. We each had a small fire extinguisher, and Taytum had also grabbed a fire blanket.

"Hey, you never know what might come in handy!" she said, slipping it into her backpack.

Towels were wrapped around our too-vulnerable necks, and sunglasses that Michelle found in the locker room protected our eyes. None of us cared to end up like Dee. In a backpack of his own, Alex was toting eight IV fluid bags, each containing a liter of 0.9% sodium chloride.

"Anyone know how many kids are currently in the oncology unit? Or how many nurses are currently working?" I asked.

"Good question. With no internet connection, I can't check. But if I remember correctly, there are usually between fifteen and twenty children, with four nurses and a couple assistants, plus a health unit coordinator during the busier hours," Taytum responded.

"We're as ready as we're ever going to be. We need to get going," Michelle said, pulling her sunglasses to the tip of her nose, and looking at us over the lenses.

"We do," Taytum said. Yet...we just stood there, looking at the medical unit that had offered a tenuous sanctuary the past few hours. We had no idea what to expect outside the walls of the fourth floor. We'd been better equipped than most, simply because we'd dealt with and learned from 'patient zero.' The other floors had no idea what was coming for them.

"Hey, wait," Michelle said, scanning the hallway. "Where's Dr. C?"

Taytum frowned. "Hm...good question. He said he was going to get something from his office and would only be a minute. Given everything that's happened, it slipped my mind, but he has been gone for a while."

"Let's get him, but we need to stay together," Alex said.

The lights briefly flickered as we made our way to the small annex off the fourth floor that housed several physicians' offices.

"That's not good," Taytum mumbled. "Last thing we need is to lose electricity too."

Michelle stopped outside a heavy oak door. A silver name plate mounted to the wall beside the door read, *Raymond V. Cherikoff, MD – Infectious Disease.*

Taytum knocked on the door. "Ray? You in there? We're heading to the pediatric oncology ward now."

No response.

She knocked again, more forcefully. "Hey, Ray…open up!"

"I don't feel good about this," I said. "We need to go in."

Taytum reluctantly nodded. After the Dee fiasco, I understood the trepidation. Slowly turning the handle, she pushed open the door.

Dr. Cherikoff was sitting in his leather chair, slumped facedown over his desk.

Alex leaned him back into his chair. His skin was cyanotic. "He's not breathing," Alex said loudly, trying to find the carotid pulse in his neck.

I lifted an eyelid. Already, his skin was cool to touch, pupils fixed and dilated. "He's gone," I said quietly, eyeing the syringe and the empty vial of morphine lying on the desk. "This was on purpose."

"Well, that's just fucking great," Michelle said, still standing by the door. "The infectious disease guy offs himself, because he sees no other way out. Not many ways to interpret that, am I right? We are *so* goddammed fucked."

"Calm down," Taytum said. "This is not a reflection of how *fucked* we are. Some people simply aren't equipped to handle such intense stress and pressure." She pulled a jacket from the coatrack and covered Dr. Cherikoff's body. "We need to return our focus to the children. But, if it's okay with all of you, I'd like us to take a few moments to compose ourselves." Then, so quietly I almost didn't hear, "Ray was my friend."

I went into the hallway and leaned hard against the wall, wanting to be alone. I did some deep breathing and a few very simple yoga poses, trying to find my center, my equilibrium. A couple minutes later, everyone joined me.

"We should take the stairs," Taytum said as we left the annex and ventured back to the fourth-floor medical ward. "After the lights flickered earlier, I started worrying about losing electricity. I sure as hell don't want to be stuck inside an elevator during this shitshow. The pediatric oncology ward is on the tenth floor. Can everyone climb six stories?" We all nodded. "Perfect. I'll lead. Alex, you take the rear. Be alert! This could get ugly fast, so have the weapon of your choice ready."

Shushing us so she could hear, Taytum peeked through a crack in the stairwell's entrance. Satisfied, she motioned us to follow. I'd seen so many horror movies, I was convinced something was going to jump out and attack us as we trudged up the stairs. Thankfully, they remained vacant. Most folks were probably still opting for the elevators.

At the eighth floor, we started hearing glass breaking and the crashing sounds of large pieces of equipment being knocked over. By the time we reached the ninth-floor landing, the heartbreaking screams of small children had joined the clamor.

The battle had started without us.

I wasn't sure I could do this. They were kids...tiny humans who hadn't had a chance to live. Frail, defenseless children whose childhoods were forever marred by a debilitating and life-threatening bitch of a disease. They'd had a shit start to life, and now they were getting a shit ending. It wasn't fair.

Alex ran to the front of the line and, without pause, shoved open the door to the tenth floor. In one hand he held the weighted pillowcase; in the other, the fire extinguisher. His plan was to take out as many as he could...and quickly. Following his lead, Taytum, Michelle, and I readied our weapons.

Taking deep breaths, we went in.

CHAPTER 21

ALEX

Being inside a hospital during an outbreak was hell. But *this* floor—the pediatric oncology unit—it could only be the seventh circle...*violence*. Brutal, unapologetic, torturous violence. Committed on and perpetrated by...*children*.

We were too late.

The hospital staff—four nurses and two assistants, as Taytum had suggested—were in a large, macabre pile behind the nurse's station. All six were partially decapitated, their heads hanging by nothing more than thin strips of sinew.

Dozens of large, purple-hued tarantulas crawled through the viscous blood accumulating beneath the corpses, leaving white egg sacks the size of my hand in their wake. Already the sacks were squirming, newborn spiders ready to break free. I'd guessed correctly. I knew what the white globules were we'd seen earlier. Delgado had been full of tarantula eggs.

"Are you seeing what I'm seeing?" Michelle asked.

I glanced at the madness playing out around us. Amongst the bright colors, the lighthearted collages, and the baby animal paintings, tiny, spider-puppeteered humans moved like malfunctioning robots. Their bodies were drenched in blood, their pearly teeth shining through crazed smiles. Vomit flowed free as more and more children succumbed to the infestation. Hundreds of tarantulas scurried around their feet, looking for new hosts...and they were coming for us.

"Yep. I see it too. We need to move, or we're going to become prime real estate for these hairy fuckers. Let's clear each room, then get the hell out of here. Michelle and I will take the front. Taytum, you and Bethany take the back. Do not feel guilty about what we must do. These kids, they're...they're already dead. Remember that."

On cue, a little boy, bald, probably no older than five, ran toward me...mouth open, throat already contracting. I swung my pillowcase hard enough to crush the side of his head. He collapsed to the ground, spider legs already protruding from his mouth. His baby teeth rubbed hairs off its carapace.

"It's trying to find a new host!" Taytum said. "Fucking thing... killing sick babies!" She stabbed it with her scalpel, as it worked its way from the boy's throat.

"Come on. We need to go. We're sitting ducks in the open." I started down the long hallway. "If there are any survivors, I'll be surprised, but we need to make sure. Keep your backs to the wall."

"Oh my God," Bethany said, voice strangled, eyes wide as she stared down the corridor.

Sitting outside nearly every patient room was a corpse...its back against the drywall, legs splayed, blood dripping.

"Are those the *parents?*" Michelle sounded pissed.

"I don't understand," Taytum said. "Why were only the adults murdered? Why weren't they used to spread the parasites...or even as hosts?"

"Probably because the parasites have already spread enough throughout the hospital to tip the scales in their favor," Bethany said. I groaned at the implication that things may have already reached the point of no return. "And probably because these adults were healthy. Too much of a fight to take them over."

We moved slowly down the hall, none of us commenting on Bethany's astute observations. In that moment, we couldn't. It was unwelcome information we needed to digest.

"The fuckers probably needed to get the adults out of the way so they could get to the defenseless kids more easily." Michelle said.

"That's likely," I agreed.

When we reached the first corpse, we took a moment to regard the poor woman's remains.

A mother.

Stressed.

Probably depressed.

Financially ruined from the endless medical bills.

Dealing with a terminally ill child...maybe on her own.

And this was her fate...

The blood on her neck was dark and tacky. She'd been dead for a while.

"Come on," I said, motioning for them to follow. "There's nothing we can do for her. She's gone. Let's just do our job and scoot. This floor is freaking me out."

"Something moved inside her neck!" Bethany said, slightly hysterical.

We all hunkered down to look. Sitting within the gaping wound were hundreds of glittering arachnid eyes.

"Ah, fuck! That's gross!" Michelle said, pulling out her fire extinguisher and blasting the foamy chemical jet inside the slashed hole. Tiny tarantula corpses streamed from the gash, their bodies torn and deformed from the force of the spray.

We cautiously entered the first room. Two little girls, both with floral scarves covering their heads, played with dolls beside the large window.

"Are they okay?" Bethany whispered.

I watched them play for a few seconds, but their backs were the only parts we could see. "Not sure. They seem fine, but...that little voice inside my head is screaming that something's very wrong."

"They seem fine," Taytum said. "The door was shut...maybe they were overlooked?" She glanced at the names written on their individual patient boards. Then, in a loud, chirpy voice, "Riley and Lily... such pretty names! How are you girls doing today?"

She took a few steps toward them, hoping they'd acknowledge her, but they continued to play with their dolls. Not together...side by side.

Taytum turned, her expression perplexed. "This is parallel play. Something toddlers do. Not seven or eight-year-olds like these two. Kinda bizarre—"

One of the girls whirled and lunged, wrapping herself around Taytum's back, while the other went for her knees, knocking her to the floor. Taytum screamed, trying to fight them off, while we gaped in horror.

The little girls weren't little girls anymore. They'd...*morphed.* Purplish hair grew from their arms and legs. Their bellies were rounded, pregnant-like. Six additional black eyes adorned their foreheads, and chelicerae—fangs—protruded from the upper gums and through their lips. Fangs that were currently puncturing Taytum's scalp and calf.

"Get them off me!" she shrieked, trying to roll onto her back. It didn't work. She was effectively pinned.

Bethany brought her loaded pillowcase down on one of the girl's heads. She roared and rolled off Taytum, then fell to the floor onto her back, her body slowly curling in on itself as she died. Michelle, free from the shock of seeing two atrociously mutated children, took Bethany's lead and hit the other. I ran to Taytum as Bethany and Michelle dispatched the two tarantulas leaving the girls' bodies.

"What happened? What did they do?" I cried, rocking her in my arms. I couldn't lose another friend. Not today. "Are you okay?"

"Ven-um," she said, choking on her saliva. Her eyes were glassy. "Too...late."

I cradled her head in my lap and stroked her hair. "I'm so sorry, Taytum."

"Hurts." Bloody tears ran down her pale cheeks. "Kill...me. Please."

"Absolutely not. We're in a hospital. There is anti-venom in the ER. We'll just run down there and..."

Michelle plunged both of her propofol syringes into Taytum's neck. "It's not enough. Give me more."

"Stop fucking around, Michelle!! You're killing her!"

Taytum was unconscious, her breathing shallow. Bethany handed Michelle her own syringes. Less than a minute later, Dr. Reznik was gone.

"She was already dead, and you know it, Alex. Like Taytum told Bethany earlier...*get it together*." Michelle walked out of the room.

Bethany looked sadly at me, then Taytum. "It had to be done, Alex. She was suffering. And what if she'd mutated? Michelle gave her the most humane death she could." Her hand grazed my shoulder just before she left.

I'm not ashamed to say I lost it then.

I cried not only for Taytum, but for Starkweather, whose wife was still waiting for him at home. I cried for a Cherikoff, a good man who'd dedicated his life to helping others. For Trudy, who was only doing her job, but was forced into the role of 'bad guy.' When all this was over, she'd only be remembered for spreading the parasite throughout the hospital. Nothing more.

I cried for all of us, because if even one got out alive, it would be a goddamn miracle.

Several minutes later, I felt better. I raided Taytum's pockets and removed her backpack, carefully transferring her supplies into my bag. With one final look at my friend, I walked out the door.

CHAPTER 22
MICHELLE

"The next three rooms are clear," I informed Alex as he came toward us. His eyes were red and swollen, but his expression was determined. "Full of blood and other nasty stuff, but empty."

"Good. Let's finish up and get somewhere safe so we can make plans."

He followed me to the next room, Bethany on his heels, when a little girl with red hair, freckles, and a fang protruding from each ear loped down the hall toward us. She was wearing an Ariel costume and a string of intestine around her neck.

Not wasting a second, Bethany twisted, her right leg extending and kicking the child in the face. 'Ariel' fell, sprawled on her back several feet away. Before I could blink, Bethany was on top of her, stabbing the tiny body viciously with her scalpel. When the puppeteering spider made its appearance, Bethany—no joke—grabbed it with her bare hands and ripped it apart, throwing hairy arachnid parts in every direction.

I gaped.

Alex gawked.

When she finished her body desecration, she checked the room.

"It's clear," she said, jogging to the next one.

"What the hell just happened?" I said.

"I think, and this is just a guess," Alex whispered, "...that Bethany might be a secret superhero."

I chuckled. "That was some serious Bruce Lee shit she threw down."

"Did you know she could—"

"Uh, guys," Bethany called out. "Come quick."

We ran to where she was standing in the room's threshold. Two children were inside. Both were crawling.

One on the ceiling. One on the window.

"This is a joke, right?" Bethany said, watching them scuttle along impossible surfaces.

"No more so than your kung fu moves," I said. Then, in a whisper, "They were hot as fuck. I'd like to see you in action again sometime."

"I'll think about it," she said, trying to smile. "I know that was a lot to witness. The girl...she just...I didn't see her as a child anymore. She was an incubator of something evil. Something that killed my friends. I was angry. I still am."

"I get it."

The child on the ceiling noticed us and started singing, "Itsy bitsy spider went up the waterspout..." His voice was raspy, and he whistled through his fangs.

"Spiders can't jump, right?" I looked up. "Because he's right above us."

"Down came the rain and *washed the spider out...*"

He landed on my shoulder, knocking me onto the bed. Wrestling the vile creature, I managed to get on top. Grabbing the leg protruding from his stomach, I launched him across the room. He hit the window, knocking the other boy/spider off. They crashed to the floor, a pile of writhing, hairy legs. Alex viciously kicked them, used his scissors to cut off their fangs, then stabbed them repeatedly with their own body parts. Blue blood oozed from the boys' wounds.

The past five minutes had me wondering—were my friends ninjas...or psychopaths?

"Michelle, you're bleeding!" Bethany examined my neck.

"I guess the towel didn't help, huh? Is it a scratch?"

She didn't say anything.

"It's that deep? Am I going to die?" I chuckled.

"You're bit," she said quietly.

"What? No way! There was no time! You saw...I threw him across the room in seconds."

I ran to the mirror over the sink. Two circular puncture wounds oozed blood just below my jawline. Seeing Bethany's devastated face in the mirror's reflection, I turned to her.

"Hey, this is fine. I feel fine! Let's not worry about it just yet. We have a job to do, so let's do it. Okay?"

"Yeah," she sniffled. "Okay." Devastation filled her voice.

Alex said nothing, just stared at the floor.

"HELP! PLEASE HELP US! IS ANYBODY THERE?"

It sounded like a little girl calling from the far end of the hall.

"I can't believe it...actual survivors!" Alex said, running to the door. "They need us!" When we didn't move, he said, "C'mon! What's your problem?"

"These children, mutations—whatever the hell they are—they can talk. This could be a trap," Bethany answered.

He looked at her like she was an idiot. "And it might not. We can't assume."

"He's right. We need to check it out," I said, stepping into the hallway. "And yes, I feel fine." I gave her a reassuring look.

"Let's do a quick scan of the rest of these rooms. We don't want any nasty surprises coming at us while we're distracted with these kids." Alex pointed to the four remaining doors.

One by one, we searched, finding a few gnarly corpses, a lot of funky gore, and way too many egg sacs...but no children. Standing outside the last door, we tried figuring out the best way to handle things.

"DID YOU HEAR THAT? I THINK SOMEBODY *IS* OUT THERE, ALYSSA! WILL YOU PLEASE HELP US? ANYBODY? HELP US! WE'RE STUCK!" This time the voice belonged to a little boy.

"Okay, I'll go in first," Alex said. "You two guard the door. When I give the 'all clear,' follow me in, and we'll figure it out from there."

"What's that noise?" Bethany asked.

"What noise?" I asked, listening. "I don't hear anything."

"That...rustling. You can't hear it?"

I shook my head.

Alex said, "I hear it. It's coming from above us."

We all looked up. The air conditioning vent vibrated briefly, just before jettisoning out of the wall, followed by a horde of spiders. They swarmed down the wall, heading right for us.

"This is so not cool," I mumbled.

"Fire extinguishers!" Alex yelled. "On my count. Three, two... NOW!" Foamy spray saturated the hallway.

"It's working!" Bethany let out a cheerful whoop, as spider bodies flew backward in broken heaps.

Thirty seconds later, the tanks were empty, and the spiders were still coming. Alex pulled the fire blanket he'd taken from Taytum out of his backpack.

"I'm going to cover as many of the fuckers as I can with this. Once I do, start stomping." He got into position. "Are you with me?"

"Yes," I said.

"Of course!" replied Bethany.

He heaved it into the air, the six-by-six blanket covering a large portion of our section of the hallway...and dozens of spiders. Without waiting, Bethany and I jumped onto the blanket. Loud crunching sounds echoed throughout the ward, as we trampled the bodies.

"Good enough. Come on, let's go." Alex motioned to the doorway, where the kids were bellowing excitedly for help. "We'll deal with the rest of them on the way out."

Sprinting into the room, Alex pulled the door shut behind us.

Big mistake.

We were caught in a massive spider web that filled the space wall to wall, ceiling to floor. Alex's immediate screams cut off abruptly when the expected web burns never came. He flailed in confusion, attempting to free himself.

"Why isn't it sizzling through our skin?"

"Hard to say," Bethany said. "Maybe only the webbing from 'patient zero' caused burns?"

"Yeah. Could be," Alex said, his relief palpable.

A child, sex indeterminable, sat in the upper corner, the spinnerets growing from its bottom shooting out glossy white webbing.

"Alex, look." I pointed. Near the center of the giant web, two silk-wrapped, swaddled kids hung helplessly. Their entire faces, except for their mouths, were covered.

"Okay, what do we have that can help us?" Alex asked.

"What about the scissors?" Bethany said, shuffling through the items in her pockets. "If we all start cutting the web's infrastructure, the cocoons will eventually drop. We can free them and get the hell out of here."

"Works for me," I said. We got to work, our efforts slowly collapsing the web.

"Holy crap, I can't believe it's actually working," Bethany said, as the cocoons dropped low enough for Alex to grab each of the children.

We carefully cut the silk away from their bodies. Two blonde, brown-eyed kids, approximately the same age, were revealed. They wobbled unsteadily as they tried to stand.

"What's your name?" I asked the girl.

It took her a moment to answer. "Alyssa. This is my twin brother, Archer."

"How old are you?" Bethany asked gently.

"We're nine, but we'll be ten in two weeks," Alyssa said.

The kids were remarkably calm, considering what they'd been through. I would've been traumatized for days.

"Why aren't you wearing hospital gowns?" I asked.

"Oh, we're not sick. Our brother is...was," Archer said sadly.

Bethany hugged him. "Is your brother gone?"

"That's him over there." Alyssa pointed to a deflated cocoon in the corner of the room. "That thing sucked him dry. His body was all shriveled up. It got our mom too, but we don't know where she is." Tears poured from brown eyes.

I had a good idea her mom was hallway decor, but I didn't mention it. "We'll get you out of here, but we need you both to listen and follow our directions carefully, okay?"

"Okay," Alyssa replied. "We're good listeners. We make straight As at school."

Archer nodded in agreement.

"Just give me a minute," Alex said. He climbed onto the bed closest the door and snipped the threads beneath the web-making creature. Sensing the instability, it scurried to the other side. "Fuck!"

"Let's just leave it," Bethany said, sounding exhausted.

"No." I said. "It's a violation of all that's good and right in the world. It needs to die." I'd already joined Alex at snipping away the webbing.

Knowing it was senseless to argue, Bethany gave Alyssa Taytum's scissors, while Archer sat quietly in a chair by the door. Together, we worked at destroying the hybrid creature. When Alex finally pulled it down, it hissed, fighting hard, but a spinal needle pushed deep into its eye ended its reign of terror.

"That's icky," Alyssa said, watching blue blood spurt from the wound.

"It sure is," Bethany said.

Raiding the room for supplies, we wrapped towels around each of the kids' necks, while Bethany and I slipped our sunglasses onto their faces.

"How're you feeling?" Bethany quietly asked.

Doing a quick body evaluation, I said, "Totally fine." I meant it too.

She studied me. "Good," she finally responded. "Hang in there, okay?"

"You know I will."

"Now, listen," Alex directed his words at Archer and Alyssa, as he passed out the bags of intravenous fluid. "There are a bunch of spiders outside. Nothing like the one in here. These are much smaller, and they're all arachnid. No human DNA mixed in, okay?"

"We know what spiders are, sir," Archer said, his innocent sarcasm making me laugh.

"Fair enough," Alex said. I could see the corners of his mouth twitching, as he struggled not to grin. "So, now that we've determined we know what spiders are, I want you to pop the plug out of this valve here. See?" He demonstrated. "When you see a spider coming at you, squirt some of this salt water on it. You don't need much, so try to conserve what you have. We need to make it up two flights of stairs to the physical therapy unit. I'm hoping we can find a safe place there to hunker down, rest, and reevaluate the situation. Alyssa and Archer, please stay as close as you can to Michelle and Bethany. They'll protect you."

Alyssa slid her hand into Bethany's, while Archer grabbed mine and squeezed.

"Okay, are we ready?"

"YES!" the children yelled excitedly.

Alex pulled open the door, looked both ways, and exited. We followed.

Spiders immediately darted toward us. The salt solution worked well, almost instantly dehydrating and killing them. We were making good time working our way down the hall, when Archer suddenly screamed.

"Get it off! Get it off me!"

A spider had crawled up his back and was hanging out between his neck and the not-so-protective towel. I showered the spider with the liquid and watched it fall to the floor, legs curling in on themselves.

"Are you okay?" I asked, but I could see he wasn't. He'd been bitten just below his jawline. Like me.

CHAPTER 23

BETHANY

As expected, the physical therapy unit was empty. When the outbreak occurred, it was nearly closing time for PT. I hoped they'd all gotten out before the quarantine. The corridors were dark and silent. Spooked, we found a large supply closet that locked from the inside and hunkered down.

I immediately got to work disinfecting and dressing the spider bites on Michelle and Archer. Alyssa held her brother's hand and cried. Already his body was wracked with teeth-rattling chills. I found a thermometer on the shelves and checked his temperature—104.3. I had no medication to offer, but there was a cold therapy machine on one of the shelves, with cooling leg compression stockings. I slipped those on him in hopes it would reduce the fever.

"Get me out of here!" he screamed.

"We have no other place to go, sweetheart," I said.

"This jungle...don't like it. Scary. Take me home!"

I ran my fingers through his hair, trying to calm him.

"Did you, uh, hear what he said, Alex?" I inquired, looking at him over Archer's sweaty head.

"I did."

"Interesting, yes?"

"Very."

Alyssa was following the conversation closely. "What? What's interesting?"

"Have you and Archer ever been to the jungle, or maybe a rainforest?"

She shrugged. "I mean, like, at the zoo."

"But you've never been to Peru or anywhere in South America?" I asked.

"Nah. Nothing like that."

"Is there any reason Archer would be having hallucinations about a jungle?"

She shrugged again. "No."

"This is some *Twilight Zone* bullshit. It sounds like he's somehow seeing Delgado's memories," Michelle said. "As if tonight couldn't get any more fucked up."

"It's all connected," Alex said. "*Somehow*, it's all connected."

While Alex stewed and Alyssa sang quietly to Archer, I focused on Michelle. "How're you feeling now?"

"Fine. I promise I'll tell you if it changes."

"I just ask that you're honest. I can't help if you aren't." My eyes were glassy and wet, as I fought off tears. The stress and outlandishness of the past few hours had taken a toll on my mental and emotional health.

"Bethany, I swear to you, I feel fine. I'm not having a single physical symptom. There are no jungle scenes flashing through my mind, I don't have a fang growing from my boob, and, as far as I know, I still only have two eyes." She crossed hers while blowing me a kiss.

Admittedly, she looked perfectly healthy. Aside from the bandage on her jaw, her eyes were clear and bright, her color was fine, she wasn't sweating, and she was being her normal, crazy self. What she said checked out.

Alex sat beside us. "I want you both to stay here with the kids while I check out this floor. It seemed benign when we arrived, but I want to try to gather information and see if I can find any useful weapons. You cool with that?"

"Sure, if you think you're safe by yourself," I said, glancing at Michelle. No way was I letting her go anywhere.

"I'll be fine. If I'm not back in thirty minutes, assume the worst, but I *will* be back." He gave us each a hug and grabbed his pillowcase, backpack, and a new fire extinguisher he found on the supply closet shelves. "Please lock the door behind me, but stay close, in case I need in quickly."

"Hey," I motioned for him to come closer. "Can you try to find some Tylenol for Archer? Maybe an oxygen tank and nasal canula?"

Alex looked sadly at the boy. "Of course."

"Thank you. I appreciate it. Please be careful."

When he left, I flipped the lock and pushed a small cart in front of the door as a barricade. It couldn't hurt.

"Do you think my brother will be okay?" Alyssa asked, staring worriedly at Archer.

"He got his bite not long after I got mine...and look at me! I'm doing fine. I bet he will too. He's just smaller, so his body needs to fight a little harder." Michelle gave her a reassuring smile.

Alyssa looked to me for verification. I nodded my agreement. In a situation like this, the truth was a cruel bitch. I studied Archer, who was cyanotic, his blue-tinged skin a sign he wasn't getting enough oxygen. As his temperature continued to elevate, I worried about febrile seizures. Things were not looking good for the boy. As a nurse, it was hard watching him suffer needlessly, but unless Alex could find some supplies, there was nothing more I could do. A particularly tragic situation when we were stuck inside a large, modern medical facility.

Reassured, Alyssa got a blanket from the linen shelf, snuggled her body against her brother's, and closed her eyes. Within minutes, her breathing had deepened.

Michelle and I moved to a quiet corner of the room so as not to disturb the children. Acting clownish, Michelle smoothed her hair and made a show of adjusting her breasts into a perkier position within her bra. "Hm," she said. "Just the two of us. Whatever shall we do?"

"Michelle, c'mon." I said, giving her a teasing shove.

"I've liked you for a long time, ya know."

"No, I didn't know." I anxiously twisted my hair. "Michelle, I..." I sighed, my nervousness preventing me from saying what needed to be said.

"It's fine. You can say it." She smiled. "I already know."

I peered questioningly at her. "Well, I've...I've never been with a woman."

"I've known for a while. You should know I'm not only a lesbian... but also a mind reader."

I didn't reply. Couldn't.

"It doesn't matter to me, Bethany. Honest. I know you're interested. I've seen the way you look at me." She scooted closer. "I think we could be good together."

"But—"

"No buts. I'll teach you everything you need to know. This isn't my first rodeo, ya know. I'll be patient. Your best friend, even. Just give us a chance, okay?" When I didn't respond, she again said, "Okay?"

"Yeah, okay. I can do that." My fingers gently tickled her forearm.

She leaned forward and touched her lips to mine. I resisted at first, recognizing this was neither the time nor place for a make-out session, but I desperately needed some reassurance. Some human closeness. I suspected Michelle did too. The kiss was warm, wet without being sloppy, and the most erotic thing I'd ever experienced in my life. Her tongue touched mine, gently at first, and then with more insistence. I leaned in, my hand caressing the curve of her hip, and...

"Archer, what...what are you doing? Stop! No! Stop it! Get off me!"

I jumped, startled by Alyssa's screams. Discombobulated,

Michelle and I ran across the room to the kids. Archer had Alyssa pinned to the floor, his legs straddling her torso, teeth sunk into the soft flesh of her face. Her screams abruptly cut off. Grabbing an industrial-sized broom that leaned against the wall, I swung it like a baseball bat against Archer's chest. He flew backward, blood dripping down his chin, as he hissed his displeasure. Alyssa's face was... gone. Slimy viscera all that remained.

"Oh my God, Archer, what did you *do*?" I looked at Michelle. "Is she dead?"

Michelle nodded, her face a portrait of despair. Before I could respond, Archer grabbed my leg, pulling me off my feet. As I fought him, blocking his bites with the broomstick, I heard Alex pounding on the door.

"Let him in, Michelle!" I screamed.

Seconds later, Alex said, "Lay flat, Bethany. I've got you." I did as I was told, watching as Archer's head twisted in a direction that was clearly not compatible with life.

I couldn't help myself. I lost it then. "I can't do this anymore." I sobbed, as the dead kid fell on top of me. "I thought I could, but I can't. They're just kids! And you nearly twisted his head off."

Alex looked at Michelle, raising his eyebrows as if to say, '*What did she expect?*' Unwilling to do any coddling, he replied, "It was that or lose you. Pretty easy decision."

Minutes later, I was nestled inside Michelle's arms, while Alex took care of the twins' bodies. When he finished, he stood over us, a contemplative look on his face, then grabbed his supplies.

"Come on. We need to talk. There's a small office behind the main desk where we'll be secure and away from...them." He glanced at the dead children over his shoulder.

When we were safely locked inside the office, Alex took a moment to gather his thoughts. I could tell by the look on his face, we weren't going to like what he had to say.

"I looked around for potential weapons, but this place is useless. Basically, a bunch of TENS units and various modality machines.

There is, however, a rooftop studio on this level...a space where they do yoga and tai chi classes. It's not the rooftop for the main portion of the building, just this side section. I went outside, staying in the shadows, hoping to see or hear something."

Michelle and I leaned against each other, listening intently.

"What I saw was a massive evacuation of the surrounding buildings, with lines of buses taking folks to safety. I saw people leaping from the hospital windows and being burned with flamethrowers as soon as they hit the ground. And...and I saw two helicopter bombers sitting on top of the parking garage."

"Wait, wait. Are you telling us they're going to bomb the hospital?" Michelle asked, voice strained.

"I think so. Probably not for a few hours. They're still prepping. These things take time to coordinate. But it's coming...and quickly. That means no more screwing around. We *have* to find a way out of here."

"Wow. Okay," Michelle said. "I've been bitten. Does that mean I'm shit out of luck? I mean, I can't in good conscience go outside if I'm going to cause some sort of outbreak."

"We'll sneak you out. Take you somewhere safe and isolated while you convalesce. It'll be fine. You'll see!" I knew I was being hopelessly optimistic, but I'd die inside these walls before I left Michelle. That silly, snarky, surprisingly gentle girl who felt like my future.

"Speaking of your bite, I haven't noticed any symptoms, Michelle. Tell us how you're feeling," Alex said.

"I feel like I always feel. Are you sure I was bitten?"

"One hundred percent. You saw the fang punctures."

"Yeah, I guess I did," Michelle said. "It's just weird that it's so different this time. When a spider got me as a kid, I was *really* sick. The doctor told my parents I probably wouldn't make it. I was in the hospital for ages. I think my organs started to shut down, but then my body magically started functioning again. I don't remember much.

Mom filled me in when I was older. It's what originally got me interested in the medical field."

Alex leapt to his feet. "You were bitten by a venomous spider?" He asked sharply, staring incredulously at Michelle.

"Uh, yeah," she said tentatively, startled by his aggression.

"Why didn't you tell us?"

"I only just remembered! I was very young and unconscious pretty much the entire time. Geez, give me a break, dude."

Alex grabbed her shoulders and shook. "Don't you see? This is *important!*"

"Hey, ease up!" I said, pushing him away and standing between them.

"Goddammit, she might have immunity! Don't you see? Michelle might be the key to fighting this infestation! It's been hours since the spider bit her, yet she has no symptoms. None! That kid, Archer, got bit around the same time, and he's already dead. Sure, physical size might be a factor...but she'd undoubtedly be symptomatic by now."

As his words sunk in, my eyes widened. *Michelle might be immune!*

"We need to get her to the lab, draw some blood for a serology test. Check her antibodies. I think the one for spider bites is the Direct Coombs' Test." Alex paced excitedly.

"We're on the twelfth floor," I said.

"Yeah? And?" He gathered some IV bags and a few more fire extinguishers.

"The lab is on the first floor. Can we make it that far?"

"Remember the helicopters I mentioned outside?" There was a finality to his words. "We don't have a choice."

CHAPTER 24
MICHELLE

Could the bite I got as a kid be the key to saving people now? I contemplated this as we made our way down the stairwell. *That'd be cool.*

Alex led us, floor by floor, as Bethany covered the rear. I—now considered precious cargo which must be protected at all costs—was tucked safely in between. Aside from a few spiders, which we blasted with salt water, the trip to the lab was proving uneventful...so far.

The countdown to detonation must have begun, but we didn't know how many hours, minutes, or seconds we had left. We were living on borrowed time. I just hoped we could find a way out...or get word to those outside that we might have actual antibodies to fight against this arachnid bullshit.

I've always hated spiders. Now I remembered why. But this...this might make my pain and suffering worth it.

"I hear something," Alex said.

Bethany pushed sweaty wisps of hair from her face. "Sounds like...moaning."

I heard it too. The moans sounded sexual. *Surely people aren't getting it on* now.

As we descended to the seventh floor, Alex's shoulders tensed, and his grip tightened around the pillowcase. "Straight ahead," he whispered.

A woman, her head and shoulders propped against the wall, was sitting in the corner of the stairwell. She was obviously pregnant, a watermelon belly outlined by the standard blue and white hospital gown. Her legs were splayed, displaying the engorged folds of her genitalia. Thick, liver-colored jelly pulsed from her vagina.

"My baby...help...me." Gore-coated hands reached for us.

"What *is* that?" Bethany said, squatting to examine the hemor-rhagic discharge. "It's not a miscarriage. At least not like any I've seen before." Then, under her breath, "Not that anything is remotely normal tonight."

Realization dawned, and with it, a sense of such revulsion, I almost puked. "Bethany, remind me again. Doesn't a tarantula liquefy its food with enzymes, then suck it up?"

"Yep. That's exactly it—"

"Jesus fuck!" I cut her off, then turned away so I wouldn't have to look at the hellish scene any longer. "I think a tarantula is feeding on her baby."

"Oh my God," Alex said, running his hands through his hair and causing tufts to stand on end. "Of course. What could be weaker than an unborn baby? Their immune systems haven't even kicked in yet. Of course these eight-legged bastards would go for the fetuses."

Hearing Bethany scream, I turned back around. The woman was birthing a tarantula. It crawled out of her vagina, through the pitiful remains of her baby, and faced Alex, daring him to make his move.

"What's it doing?" he asked, unnerved. "This is new behavior. I haven't noticed the spiders being so...bold."

"It's creeping me out," I said.

The once-pregnant woman rose clumsily to her feet, her belly wilted. The tarantula at her feet never took its eyes off Alex.

"It's like a damn guard dog," he said, the tension in his voice clear.

"Please...come...closer. Need...help," she said, breathlessly. Her sagging breasts leaked bloody milk. "Save...my...baby."

Alex backed away from the woman and her spider. "What the fuck do I do?"

"She's infected, Alex. Kill her!"

He nodded, reaching for his pillowcase. Before he could act, the woman lunged, squeezing her contaminated breast milk at his face. Alex spat and sputtered, dropping his weapon and frantically wiping the fluid from his skin.

The bones in her face made loud popping sounds as they fractured. Like a python, an unhinged jaw allowed her mouth to expand to unnatural proportions. A spider leapt from the cavernous hole, attaching itself onto Alex's face. His startled screams reverberated through the stairwell.

"Holy shit!" Bethany yelled, bashing at the woman's back with her loaded pillowcase. When she clumsily turned, Bethany covered her face in pepper spray.

Alex fell to the ground.

I grabbed the 'guard' spider and smashed it against the wall. The squishing sounds were more satisfying than I could have ever imagined. Slimy entrails smeared the cement blocks before gravity won out and the spider dropped to the floor.

Pulling out a bag of IV fluid, I squirted it at Alex's face. The tarantula's shriveled, desiccated body rolled onto the woman's oozing corpse. Bethany had done a fine job putting the poor woman out of her misery.

"She had two inside her!" Bethany panicked. *"Two!"*

"Let's take care of Alex, and then we'll talk about it, okay?"

But our friend was dead.

And his eyes were missing.

Each socket contained a white circular ball.

Bethany glanced at Alex's face and stoically said, "Those are sperm packs. Mature male tarantulas pull them from their genitals, hold them in their pedipalps, and release them, *normally*, inside a female's gonopore. It's a little opening—"

"That's enough." I swallowed a mouthful of bile. "I don't need to hear more. These fucking, piece-of-shit tarantulas turned our friend into a goddamned pussy before they killed him. I am *not* okay with that."

"Do we need to..." Bethany looked broken, staring at Alex's body. "...you know, finish it?" Sobs overtook the final words.

I couldn't believe my life had come to this, but it was a necessary evil. Without responding to Bethany, I bought my pillowcase down on Alex's head. One...two...three times. Until those fucking sperm packs were nothing but ground-up goo. I knew I should be sad, but I didn't have it in me. I was too *pissed*.

Walking down the next flight of stairs, I said, "That tarantula can take his sperm packs and stick them straight up his spidery ass!"

"Spiders have an anus."

"Fine, Bethany. He can stick them up his spidery anus."

CHAPTER 25
TRUDY

Cold, safe.
You're in a box.
Not box...metal hole in wall.
Looks like a box to me.
It's...oh, mind strain...it's...morgue cabinet.
For rotting dead bodies?
Yeah, but I naked and bloody. Look dead. Safe.
You should be back in the jungle.
Ah. Jungle. So green.
So much prey.
Lots prey here too.
When are you getting out?
Work hard. Rest.
Time to finish them off.
Who?
The others. The humans. The prey.
Yes. Short rest. Hurt throat.
Fine. Sleep in your disgusting morgue hole.
Will.

What's wrong with your throat?
Vomit. Much.
You're a disappointment.
You. Asshole. Do sleep now.
You'll regret saying that.

…

…

…

Trudy?
Trudy?

CHAPTER 26

BETHANY

T he door to the medical lab was barricaded, but once we'd answered a series of questions—I guess to prove we were still human—we were allowed entrance.

"Sorry about that. Can't be too careful right now. I'm Jude." He didn't offer his hand.

Jude was a petite, shockingly thin guy with dark hair parted to the side and thick glasses. He reminded me of Herbert West from *Re-Animator*.

"I'm Bethany, and this is Michelle."

"So, not trying to be rude, but that bandage on Michelle's jaw is making me nervous. Explain, please." He backed away from us.

"That's why we're here. You see, Michelle was bitten hours ago, but she's had no symptoms. We kept waiting for something to happen, but she hasn't changed...physically, mentally, or emotionally."

"Uh, I think you both should leave."

"Please, hear us out," I pleaded.

Michelle stepped forward. "Look, when no symptoms mani-

115

fested, I suddenly remembered I nearly died as a small child after an unknown spider bite."

Jude shook his head, backing farther away.

"I can show you the scar!" Michelle pulled up the left leg of her scrub pants and displayed the lateral ankle. The skin there was rough and uneven. I guessed the venom had caused some necrosis at the time. All these years later, it was still pink and raw looking But within the mess of scar tissue, two elevated circles were obvious. "The fangs penetrated there," she offered, pointing to the area. "I'm not making this up, I swear. It's just been a part of my body for so long, I don't remember it's there anymore. We think I might be immune to whatever is happening here; that maybe there are antibodies inside me that can save other lives. Please, I'm begging you. Will you help us?"

Jude said nothing.

Desperate, I said, "We're running out of time. *All* of us. Trust me on this. Is there anyone here who might be willing to work with us?"

"I'm the only one left," Jude said.

"Then we need you, Jude. Don't let us down. Don't let *humanity* down."

As cheesy as the line was, it's the one that finally worked.

Considering, he finally said, "Come on back. The test is rarely ordered because spider bites aren't common in Duluth. They don't like the cold much. But I'm pretty sure I have the kit you need."

"Thank you, Jude," I said. "You know...for trusting us."

He gave a quick nod of acknowledgement, then entered a room barely large enough for the three of us to squeeze inside. "You," he pointed to Michelle, "...sit. I'll be right back."

When he'd drawn several vials of blood, he told us to give him an hour to "fill in the blanks." Whatever that meant.

"Any windows in here?" I asked, looking around the large wing of the hospital where the lab was located. "It would be nice to know if we're going to be blown to smithereens in the next ten seconds."

"Would it, though? Be nice, I mean?" Michelle said. "I think I'd rather be blissfully unaware."

"Yeah," I said, sighing. "I suppose you're right. I'm just very much over tonight."

"Ha! You and me both."

"Alex is dead. Taytum is dead. Dee is dead...and good riddance. Two other physicians. And poor Trudy. Who knows what happened to her." I wasn't a smoker but wished for a cigarette at that moment. "So many people lost because of Delgado." Not wanting to focus on our grim reality, yet unable to think of anything else, I said, "Ya know, there's a very good chance neither of us will be alive when the sun rises."

"Yes, I know." Michelle glanced around the space. "So let's check some of these desk drawers. Maybe we can find ourselves some liquid refreshment. Make croaking off a little more palatable."

"Why, that's a right fine ideer you have there, purty little thing." I wasn't sure what had gotten into me—pardon the pun—but I sounded like an actor on the *Hatfields & McCoys* miniseries.

"Bethany!" Michelle couldn't stop laughing. "Where did that voice come from? Should we be making moonshine instead?"

"I just figured a little stress relief was in order." I said, blushing.

Still giggling, Michelle said, "It worked. Well done, girl. Well done."

We hit the jackpot while searching the third desk. A brand-new bottle of vodka was hidden beneath a spiral-bound manual filled with lab values. A half-filled jug of orange juice sat unused inside the staff lounge fridge, so that became our mixer.

"Screwdrivers. Seems somehow appropriate tonight, doesn't it?" Michelle said, sipping her cocktail. "Since we're pretty damn *screwed*."

"Instead of sitting here getting sloshed, should we try to find a way out? I'm antsy, and this doesn't feel terribly productive."

"Not at all. If we're going to get out, we need to give them a reason not to shoot us. This is not wasted time." Michelle took another drink. "Just keep your fingers crossed I have immunity."

"Why in the world would you want to get out? This lab is secure.

We're safe here until they clear the hospital and rescue us," Jude said, strolling into the room. "My co-workers tried to leave, and they were shot like cattle. I figure, with the fridge and vending machines, I have enough food for a while. I'll wait it out."

"They're gonna blow up the hospital," a tipsy Michelle said, followed by a burp and giggle.

"What are you talking about?" Jude asked, skin pale in the bright lighting.

"Our friend, Alex, who is no longer with us..." I quickly crossed myself. "...did some snooping. He discovered they're evacuating all the nearby buildings, and he saw two helicopter bombers parked outside."

"Alex from the ER?" Jude asked.

"Yes."

"Oh, man. He's dead too? We were buddies. Was he certain?" Jude fell into a nearby chair. Exhaling dejectedly, he said, "It's Alex. Of course he was certain. He was the most thorough, dedicated, genuinely kind person working at this hospital. His poor little girl. I think she just turned three. What a blow."

"Alex had a daughter?" I asked.

"Yeah. Matilda. She was his life."

"I had no idea. I only just met him today, but we went through so much together, it felt like I'd known him forever. But I didn't. I didn't really know him at all. He never mentioned Matilda."

"He was a great guy, but private. Honest to a fault. If he said they're planning to blow this hospital up, I'd have no reason to question him."

"That's why we're hoping Michelle is immune. We need leverage with these bastards, so they'll let us out before that happens."

"She is," Jude said quietly. "That's what I came out to tell you. She's got an extraordinary number of antibodies. I think she could be bitten and puked on endlessly, and she'd still be fine."

"Oh my God! Did you hear that, Michelle? This's fantastic news!" I pulled her into my arms for a clumsy hug.

He continued, "I've never seen anything like it. Do you know what kind of spider bit you?"

"Not a clue. I was young. It was traumatic. Mom gave me only the most general details. None of us wanted to relive it. We were on vacation that summer, *that* I know, but I couldn't tell you where. I think it may have been a foreign country though, because my doctors had accents." Michelle poured herself another screwdriver and held up the glass. "Here's to a plethora of weird fuckin' antibodies!"

"Fair enough," I said. "I don't blame you or your family. I'm sure it was a horrible time. Who knows? Maybe you were bitten in Peru, maybe you weren't. It doesn't matter. What *does* matter is your current bite is a moot point."

Looking confused, Jude asked, "Peru?"

"The jungles of Peru are where all this originated, the spider hitching a ride with my patient. Also known as Alex's former ER patient. He'd been in Peru for weeks, looking for or studying...*something* with eight legs."

"Huh," Jude said.

"'Huh' what?" Michelle asked.

"It's just that..."

"What, Jude? Give us the goddamn four-one-one already." Michelle probably needed to stop drinking.

"Several of the contaminated people I saw tonight rambled incoherently about the jungle. The Peru thing is interesting information, that's all."

"Oh my God, that's right! Archer did that too! Remember, Michelle? He was hallucinating about the jungle, but Alyssa had no idea why." My mind was spinning.

"Why the jungle?" Michelle asked, suddenly sober.

"Hm. Dunno," Jude said. "But off the top of my head...maybe a mind meld? A telepathic communion? A consciousness merge? Or hell, maybe we have ourselves a good old collective consciousness."

"But what does that mean?" I asked.

"It's when a group of people, for whatever reason, share

conscious thought, sometimes a very specific one. Maybe because they're all infected, maybe because the sickness all came from the same source...who knows? It's just a guessing game at this point."

"But is it?" Michelle asked "We know this entire outbreak started from one patient who was infected by a single hellspawn tarantula. Yet, when Dr. Reznik autopsied the body, we found loads of webbing inside him, but no spider. Delgado infected Trudy, but he just puked on her...got the eggs into her system. The spider must have still been inside him at that point."

"So, where did it go?" I asked. "Do you think it's still somewhere on the fourth floor?"

"Oh. Oh, *shit!* I think I know where it ended up." Michelle stood. "Hurry. Get your gear. We need to go."

I started throwing things into a backpack.

"You too, Jude," Michelle said, looking him up and down.

"What? No way! I told you I'm staying right here."

"So you can go out in a blaze of glory when the hospital explodes?" She stood with her hands on her hips, glaring. "Is that the way you want to go? Sitting alone in a lab like a coward?"

Jude bit his lip but said nothing.

"We need your help. Stand your ass up and gather any weapons you might have. Capiche?" Unwilling to argue with a feisty Michelle, he jogged toward an office and disappeared inside.

"There's nothing but needles down here," I said, worriedly.

"Yeah, I noticed that." She put the vodka into her bag. "We can't even get more propofol here. But we still have Alex's backpack, so we're not completely fucked."

Jude returned, carrying his own crossbody bag. He handed Michelle two vials of her blood, which she tucked into her bra. "I don't have scalpels, but I have a ton of box cutters."

"Perfect. Do you have any fire extinguishers? We've found they work well against hordes of spiders."

He thought for a moment. "We do. Just trying to remember where they all are." Running off again, he was back less than a minute later, carrying two large extinguishers. "*And* I found these in the employee bathroom." He proudly held up a pair of fuzzy pink handcuffs.

"Um, what are you lab freaks doing down here, anyway?" Michelle grabbed the handcuffs and placed them inside her backpack. "Hey," she said, responding to my pointed look, "you never know what might come in handy!"

"Heh. You said 'handy.'" Jude laughed uproariously at his joke, going so far as to slap his knee.

"So I did," answered a bemused Michelle. "Okay, at some point tonight, our sunglasses disappeared, and the neck towels were piss-poor protection, so we'll just go as we are."

"We have anti-fog face shields here. We could wear a standard blue cloth mask—cover our mouths and noses—beneath it." He shrugged. "Might help."

"I like it. Let's do it," Michelle said.

When we were ready, Jude took one final look around the lab, blotted at his eyes with a tissue, then locked the door behind us.

CHAPTER 27
JUDE

I didn't know where we were going or what we were doing, and I didn't really care. I just wanted to get home to my cat, Beaker, my favorite television program, *Doctor Who*, and my video games. The two nurses seemed to know what they were doing. I hope it wasn't a mistake hitching my wagon to theirs.

CHAPTER 28

MICHELLE

We made it back to the fourth floor just as the electricity cut out. There was no flickering on and off. It was just gone. Eerie red lights sputtered to life, lining the hallways, as the generators' engine kicked on. Visibility was shit, and the timing could not have been worse. It seemed all we'd done earlier to protect our patients was for naught. Dozens of prone bodies were sprawled throughout the hallway, scurrying spiders everywhere. The staff lounge, where we'd taken patients to safety, was empty.

"I don't understand." Bethany couldn't contain her dismay. "What happened?"

I grabbed a flashlight from the drawer beside the refrigerator and shined it around the room. When the light illuminated the crusty, red bathroom, I groaned.

There was our answer.

"All those white globules we saw in the blood hatched."

"Oh, God." Bethany's hand covered her mouth in shock. "We didn't know. We couldn't have. At the time, we were doing the best we could with the information we had," she said, wrapping her arms around my waist.

125

"Fuck!" I punched the wall. It hurt like hell, but I didn't care. "Those people trusted us, goddammit!"

"We can't blame ourselves for this, Chelle. We tried."

I'd always hated that nickname, but from her, it was a sweet caress.

"Hey, uh, guys?" Jude cut in. "I don't mean to be a dick about this, but if they cut the electricity, I'm guessing our time is limited."

He was right. Using the fire extinguishers to spray the spiders away, we attempted to make our way down the hall, which was difficult because the *human* bodies were so distracting. Something freaky was happening to them. Each was on its back, legs protruding into the air. There was zero movement, and I could tell their skin was hard...shell-like. They looked like mannequins.

"Oh, man. That's Mrs. Jones," Bethany pointed to a body. "And there's Mr. Schmidt!"

"But why are they like this? Just...lying there like that?"

"I mean..." Bethany shrugged but didn't finish the sentence.

"What do you know?"

"This position they're all in, it looks like what tarantulas do when they're molting," she explained. "They have exoskeletons—basically a rigid, protective armor—which they eventually outgrow. When the exoskeleton gets too small and becomes restrictive, he tarantula molts to accommodate their increasing size. Like a snake shedding its skin. They usually molt lying on their back or side, legs in the air. Eventually, they work their way out, but they're vulnerable for a while. The new skin eventually hardens, forming a larger—more comfortable—exoskeleton."

"So, you're telling me these bodies—people we know—are too big for their skin? They're growing?"

"That's my best guess," she said. "But I honestly have no idea what will come out. Their skin...it's hiding monsters inside."

"Okay, that settles it. I'm not sticking around to fight giant humans with fangs," I said. "We need to do our job and get the hell out of here."

"What is our job? You still haven't told us. I have no idea why we're back here."

"I'm a bit curious myself," Jude said, spraying foam at more spiders.

"We know there was a spider in Delgado's body, right?"

"Correct."

"We know that it wasn't there during Taytum's autopsy."

"Correct."

"Which means it found another host somewhere on this floor."

Bethany hesitated. "Likely, yes."

"Tell me...who was attacked and controlled, even though she was inside a locked office and had minimal patient contact?"

"Oh my God! Dee! It went in through her orbital socket!"

"Bingo. And I think if we kill the original, because of their 'mind meld'"—I did air quotes with my fingers—"all its clones will die too. At least that's my hope. So, here's what we're going to do—Jude, you're going to open the door, I'm going to zap Dee with the fire extinguisher to knock her off-balance, and Bethany, you're going to handcuff her. Then we're going to cover her head with a pillowcase, put her in a wheelchair, and take her to the operating room."

"Yeah, that's right. My handcuffs for the win!" Jude said, strutting...his thin body reminiscent of a dancing *Napoleon Dynamite*.

I countered, "*Yours*, eh?"

Bethany, ignoring our banter, said, "The OR? Why?"

"I need her in a contained space."

"All right, then." She asked nothing more.

I grinned. Trust in a relationship was so important.

Standing outside Dee's office, I handed Jude the door key and Bethany the handcuffs. "I won't let her hurt you," I whispered into her ear.

Taking my place, I watched as Jude pushed the door open. Dee lurched around the room, her body in a far worse state than when we'd last seen her.

The remaining human eye bulged from its socket, while seven

new ones were arranged strategically around her face. The spider leg protruding from her head had been joined by two more. Her eyelashes—and the rest of her body hair—were purple and coarse. She no longer had teeth. Instead, two black fangs protruded from her nostrils.

And I swear she kept checking her phone.

On her deathbed, mutated into a spider-freak, looks vanished forever...and all she cared about was Chad. Or Brad. Or maybe Thad.

"Why isn't *she* molting?" Bethany whispered.

"Don't know, don't care." I sprayed her with the fire extinguisher.

She fell backward, her deformed head hitting against the desk. While she struggled to stand back up, Bethany cuffed her hands behind her back, and Jude slipped two pillowcases over her misshapen skull. A third was used to secure them around her neck, hopefully sealing in anything that might wish to come out.

"Bring in the wheelchair," I demanded.

There, we ran into an unforeseen problem. Dee's body wouldn't bend into a sitting position. Her bones, ligaments, and muscles had morphed to such an extent, it wasn't impossible.

"Okay, plan B. Let's get a body bag. We'll *drag* her bitchy ass down the stairs."

"On it!" Bethany ran from the room.

I kept my eye on Dee. She was pitiable. Aside from the monstrous head, her arms and legs looked like they'd been sewn on backward, and her belly was hugely rounded, gestational.

I'd started to tell Jude to avoid narcissistic partners—like Dee—at all costs, until I heard Bethany's distant, despairing yelp.

"Stay here," I told him. "Keep your eye on her, and do *not* let her move under any circumstances."

Bethany stood in the middle of the hallway, surrounded by the once inert bodies. Bodies which were now rocking aggressively back and forth. "They're breaking out!" she said, her voice a mixture of horror and excitement.

"Don't just stand there! Bring me the body bag!"

Hardened abdominal skin split around the sides and was pushed upward by a pair of long, segmented legs.

"The arms will come out next, followed by the head," Bethany said. "I have no idea what obscenity is being birthed, Michelle, and I'm not sure I want to. Let's get Dee and go."

We frantically wrestled her into the black bag, which was not easy given her contorted body, and drug her into the hallway. A creature, at least eight-feet tall, was slowly lumbering through the unit. Its skin was hairless and pink, throbbing with large blue blood vessels. There weren't eight eyes, but one huge one in the center of its... *forehead?*

"Holy shit, it's Mr. Casper!"

"Is it blind?" I asked as it walked face-first into the wall.

"No," said Bethany. "During the molting process, it sheds its eyes too...so they're basically brand new. Right now, his skin is soft and fragile, and he's exhausted. Plus, it takes time to get used to the new duds."

"Should we kill him?"

"There isn't time." The sound of helicopter engines roared in the distance. Bethany looked at the rest of the rocking bodies. "They'll all complete their molts in the next few minutes. We need to go."

"You're right. We need to take care of this brainless shrew and get the hell out of dodge."

The three of us grabbed a portion of the bag near Dee's head and dragged her toward the stairwell.

"Michelle?" Jude tentatively asked as we made our way to the second floor, Dee's lower body thudding against each step.

"Yeah?"

"If the building is going to be a massive fireball in the next hour, why are we even bothering with Dee?"

"Because what if she survived and got loose? I believe her spider is the mastermind. It needs to die."

"That's fair," he said, gasping for breath as he pulled Dee's writhing body. "Man, she's not light, is she?"

"She does seem oddly...stout," Bethany agreed.

"We're almost there," I said, exhausted myself. It had been a hell of a night. When we reached the doors to the operating rooms, I pulled out my badge, holding it against the wall mounted scanner. Nothing happened.

"No electricity," Jude reminded me, snickering.

"Yeah, well, suck it," I said, pushing the door open.

The OR was full of molting bodies.

"Just ignore them and follow me. Hurry. Pretty sure we're out of time."

We dragged Dee's body into the first suite we came to. I flipped the light switch and nearly cheered when the room lit up. I knew the OR had an isolated power system. They obviously couldn't lose electricity in the middle of a surgical procedure, so all the rooms were outfitted with special, independently operated electrical panels.

The floors were concrete, the tables metal, and the cabinets a metal/glass combination...it was just what I needed. I wasted no time getting to work. All supplemental oxygen sources, provided for anesthesia to maintain patient airways, were turned on, letting the rich oxygen flow freely into the room's atmosphere. Dee was placed on the OR table, her arms strapped to the arm boards, legs secured inside stirrups. A sterile drape covered her grotesque body.

"What in the world? Are we doing *actual* surgery?" Bethany sounded perplexed and vaguely annoyed that she still didn't know my plans.

I pulled the bottle of vodka from my backpack and poured it onto the drapes and Dee's cotton-encased head.

Bethany stepped back. "Oh," she said, finally understanding.

"Alex saw the soldiers using flamethrowers on all the folks who managed to get out of the hospital. They know something we don't. Fire is key. So, I'll be removing Dee and her passenger from existence."

"But...the oxygen, the alcohol...you're going to blow us all up!"

"No, I'm not. You'll see."

All the operating suites in the hospital had swinging doors on both the north and south facing walls. I locked the south facing door, stuffing wet towels into the gap, then pulled the electrocautery machine toward Dee.

"Bethany, Jude...head for the exit. I'll join you shortly."

"I'll wait in the hallway, thanks." Bethany stomped angrily to the door. "And quit being a bossy bitch."

I couldn't help it...I laughed. Bethany was everything I wasn't and, God help me, I loved her.

I used the mobile x-ray wall to protect myself from errant flames, rearranged everything so I had easy access, depressed the button on the electrocautery pencil, or the Bovie, and touched it to the alcohol-soaked drapes. Combined with the oxygen rich environment, I had created the perfect fire triad. The drapes ignited. I dropped the Bovie onto Dee's head and backed toward the door, pushing through just as the supplemental oxygen caused a significant explosion.

My body sailed several feet through the air before plopping unceremoniously onto Bethany's feet.

"Brilliant," she said, voice dripping sarcasm.

Jude helped me up. Dizzy, I stumbled back to the suite's entrance, making sure the body was charred...that nothing was still alive.

What I saw was a crispy body, flaming hair, and a slightly burnt—but very much alive—tarantula scampering toward the hallway.

"It's coming! Stop it!" I screamed. All that work, yet I'd only managed to put that hag, Dee, out of her misery.

Over the next few minutes, I learned two things:

1. Tarantulas are fast little fuckers.
2. I need to get my ass to the gym more often.

The three of us chased it down several dimly lit corridors and stairwells, finally cornering it in the most unappealing place of all—the *morgue.*

CHAPTER 29
TRUDY

You. Here?
They're trying to kill me. I need you.
Much rest. Can. Help.
I'm leading them to you. Be ready.
So ready.

CHAPTER 30

BETHANY

I *really* didn't want to go into the morgue. Like...really, really. But the tarantula headed directly to the basement, a predictable place for an arachnid, and we followed. I simply wasn't expecting to enter the chilled, temporary resting place of the dead. It was silly, I know. I'd seen dozens of dead bodies tonight—it shouldn't be a big deal. But something about the morgue—the unnatural silence, the briskness of the air, the *smell*—it was all just so disconcerting and...*ick*.

The room was pitch black. No red lights in here. The residents didn't require them. Michelle flicked on the flashlight. The single cool, white beam showed the cooler—cabinet after cabinet of cadaver storage—and little else. Autopsies were not conducted here. This was nothing more than the death depot. Membership meant a brief respite until the medical examiner or funeral home picked them up.

I noticed an open cabinet door. It was empty...but I was still creeped out.

"There it is!" Jude shouted, dashing toward the far corner of the room.

The light jerked as Michelle headed in that direction, so I didn't see what happened. I only heard Jude's scream. The acoustics in the room were off, they had to be, because he sounded far away.

"Shit, where did it go?" Michelle asked, doing frantic zoomies with the light. I guess she figured she'd worry about Jude *after* the tarantula was dispatched. A second later I heard, "What the...?" The flashlight clattered to the cement floor as something...*someone*... attacked Michelle.

Jude was nowhere to be seen, Michelle was grunting as she fought whatever monstrosity had attacked her...and I could do nothing to help either of them. Because, at that moment, something large and hairy crawled up my leg. I shrieked and fell backward, landing hard on my hip.

"It's on me! The God spider is on me!" I relentlessly tried brushing it away with my hands, but it was too big. Too strong. Too *determined*. It needed a host, and I was the prime candidate.

Meanwhile, on the other side of the room...

"Trudy, it's me, Michelle! Your *friend*."

This, and then...the crack of a breaking bone.

A weird keening sound.

The splatter of bloody, egg-infested vomit bathed in the light of the abandoned flashlight.

"Jesus fuck, that's gross! And seriously, could your breath be any worse? Kinda feel like I'm gonna vomit myself now. How would you like it if I blew my lunch all over you, ya filthy freak?"

Michelle had a way with words.

The spider was now sitting on my chest. I really hoped she finished Trudy off soon. And where the hell was Jude? My hip was a mass of white-hot agony as I used a cabinet door to pull myself upright. The tarantula's pedipalps were hungrily exploring the contours of my neck. I tried knocking it off again, going so far as to smash it between my breasts and the metal doors, to no avail.

It really was a God spider.

"Sorry for you, your explosive digestive display has no effect on me. I'm immune, ya squalid bitch," Michelle said, conversationally.

"And frankly, I've had just about enough of you." I heard a series of vertebrae popping...

...followed by a gurgling sound.

...followed by a body thudding to the ground.

...followed by the crunch of a foot coming down on a large spider.

Jude called from somewhere...*below?* "Hey, guys? I'm hurt pretty bad. And there's a dead body down here, but I think I might have found a way out."

"In a minute, Jude!" Michelle called out as she grabbed the flashlight and started toward me. The rhythmic thrumming of helicopter's rotor blades became significantly louder.

"Hurry!" I shrieked. "Kinda desperate here."

The spider, who'd been chill until then, picked that moment to strike. His fangs sunk so far into my neck, I worried they'd come out the other side. My entire world—entire *being*—

filled with pain so exquisite, it was all I could see, hear, feel. I fell onto a morgue table, and the tarantula followed. I did my best to get away, scooting inside the cabinet despite my shattered hip, but it proved futile. The tarantula hissed, its upper body raised into a threat pose, just before attacking again. This time its fangs sank into my chest, just above my heart.

"Bethany, no!" Michelle screamed, as the first of many explosions shook the building.

"Guys? You'd better come now! That, uh, didn't sound so good," Jude called.

We ignored him.

"I'm going to kill that sadistic fucker, then pull you out. We'll get out of here, and you'll be just fine." Michelle said, her eyes ripe with fear. And maybe sadness. They already told the story she hadn't yet admitted to herself.

It was too late for me.

Venom coursed through my body, and unlike Michelle, I didn't have antibodies. Already, my breathing was labored, heart thudding erratically inside my chest. I hurt everywhere and fervently wished for some propofol, like we'd given Taytum.

Explosion after explosion rocked the building.

"Shut the door and go, Michelle. Save yourself," I whispered as the spider sank his fangs into my stomach. "Please."

"No."

Jude's voice was shrill. "Come now! It's our only chance!"

"I'm begging you. Leave me. My body is shutting down. I can't move. Please, just close the door. Lock this bastard in here and run. Get out as fast as you can. You still have a chance."

I couldn't see Michelle's face, but I could hear her sobs. "Bethany, please...*please* don't make me do this."

"I've blindly trusted you through all this, haven't I? Now it's your turn to trust me. Please, just...shut the door."

"I'll never forget us," she said, her voice so quiet I almost didn't hear. The door closed, and I was alone.

Darkness had weight.

CHAPTER 31
MICHELLE

I was numb, emotionless. Working on autopilot, I shined the flashlight in the direction of Jude's panicked voice and saw a trapdoor in the floor. It was open. Jude, blind in the pitch-black confines of the morgue, must have fallen in.

Another explosion rattled the hospital. I needed to escape. I tried not to think. I tried to erase images from my mind...

Images of Bethany lying in a suffocatingly cold, dark, smelly morgue cabinet.

Images of a tarantula feeding on her living body.

Images of the building collapsing around her as she lay all alone in the darkness.

A loud wail, filled with absolute misery and heartbreak, released from the depths of my core as I started down the crumbling stairs, pulling the heavy trapdoor closed behind me.

A body, its neck torqued, stretched across the bottom stair. At first, I thought it was Jude. Then I saw him curled into the fetal position about twenty feet farther down the tunnel. Wondering how the dead guy knew about this passageway—when no one else did—I made my way to a blubbering Jude.

"Get up! We need to get as far away from the hospital as we can." My tone was sharp. I had no patience for weakness, especially after Bethany's sacrifice.

"Okay," he sniffled, "but I hurt my ankle when I fell. Not sure I can walk."

"Dammit, Jude! Fucking try! You want to live, don't you?" Tears covered my face, and my words were staccatoed as I gasped and hiccupped through my grief.

"Where's Betha—"

"Don't. Do *not* say her name." I jogged down the tunnel.

"Don't leave me, please. I'm so sorry. I didn't know." He sounded pitiful, terrified...like a little boy. I heard his uneven shuffles behind me as he tried to keep up.

Feeling like a gigantic dick—none of this was the kid's fault—I stopped and waited for him to catch up, then offered my arm. He took it gratefully, and we made our way down the snake-like turns of the tunnel.

"I really hope this flashlight doesn't die," I said, just before a thunderous boom knocked us off our feet.

Metal creaked and groaned. Chunks of dirt and concrete, dislodged from the tunnel's surface, pummeled our vulnerable bodies. My lungs felt heavy from the smoke and dust, wracking my body with paroxysmal coughs so violent, I vomited. Bitter bile coated my mouth, as did the aftermath of the sulfurous debris.

Then, ghastly silence.

We laid curled together in the inky tunnel, flashlight shattered beyond repair.

It was then it hit me...

I lived in a world without Bethany.

She was gone.

I gripped Jude tighter.

CHAPTER 32
JUDE

We stayed there for hours.

Days.

Weeks.

Hell, I don't know. Time lost all meaning in the opaque shadows.

The explosion damaged our eardrums. It took a long time to hear words coming from moving lips.

I thought endlessly of my cat, Beaker. I just wanted to go home. Call my mom. Get a hot shower. Be the Jude I was *before* the tragedies of this night.

"You can't go home," Michelle said, seemingly reading my thoughts. "At least not for long."

"What do you mean I can't go home?"

"You and I both know there is a master list of every single person inside that hospital...the patients, the personnel, even the visiting public. According to the government, we're officially dead, and that's just the way they want it. If we suddenly show up alive and well, they will hunt us down, and they *will* kill us. We've seen their solution to this problem, and it ain't quarantine," she said matter-of-factly. "When we get out of this tunnel, you need to find a discreet way back to your house, get only what you *need*—don't make it obvious belongings are missing—and get the hell out of town. Don't call your family, your friends, your lovers...not a soul, Jude. Lay low, change your name, and this one is important...do *not* continue working in the medical field."

"But what else can I do? That's all I know. I have no skills or talents." I sounded whiny, and I knew I sounded whiny.

"Jesus, Jude, who gives a fuck? You're alive...isn't that all that matters? Now get up. It's time to go."

We were both beaten, battered, and scared silly. The struggle as we made our way through those endless tunnels was mighty. At times, I carried her. Other times, she carried me. She seemed unaware of the tears that streamed endlessly down her grimy cheeks.

When we finally reached the longed-for door, neither of us knew what to do. I looked at her. She looked at me. We looked at the door, then back the way we came. The one thing we were sure of...the tunnels were our haven. We were safe there. The other side of the door brought only the unknown. Were we ready to face a world where everything looked and felt different?

There wasn't a choice.

We could have opened the door to a torrent of bullets, had dogs sicced on us, or walked into the sizzling heat of a flamethrower...but that's not what happened. Instead, we found ourselves in the sub-basement level of a parking garage, several miles from the hospital. We had no transportation, no phones, no money...so we did the only thing we could.

Hugged and went our separate ways.

"Hey, Jude?" she said, as I limped away.

I turned. "Yes?"

She pulled the vials from her bra and threw them to the ground. They shattered, spattering the cement with crimson blood.

Her cure.

"We won't be needing those now," she said, offering a small smile, then disappearing into the shadows.

That's the last time I saw her.

Though I still see her and Bethany in my dreams.

EPILOGUE
DR. ROSALIE DOWD

Authorities are calling the incident that took the lives of over twelve-hundred people, both patients and employees, at Superior Life Medical Center yesterday, a 'necessary evil.' Roger Eaton, spokesman for the Center for Disease Control, said the virulent supervirus brought to the area by Dr. Francisco Delgado, a scientist recently returned from South America, was so aggressively contagious that, had it reached the general population, eighty percent of Duluthians would have expired within twelve hours.

::*Video clip of Roger Eaton:*::

"I cannot stress this enough. Had the National Guard not acted as quickly and efficiently as they did, far more lives would have been lost. This wasn't an easy decision, but it was the right one."

And that was Roger Eaton, spokesman for the Center for Disease Control.

We've been told more information is forthcoming. In the mean-

time, a list of those lost can be found on the CDCs website. Duluth's mayor, Cynthia Olsen, said therapists will be working around the clock at the courthouse for the next week to help survivors, and their families, process this unimaginable tragedy.

I'm Lorna Lucas, and that's it for the News at Noon. We'll see you back here at five o'clock for the evening edition of KBJR News. Have a good day, Duluth!

I shut off the television. A virulent supervirus, my ass. Francisco was my employee, my lover, he was in Peru under my orders, and I was the one who'd notified the authorities when I found out he was a patient in the hospital. My staff kept them abreast of the situation while he was in South America, so when I called yesterday afternoon with the urgent update, they were ready to mobilize. In my heart, I knew his hospital visit could mean nothing good for the city or the people who lived here.

I stared out the bay window as I sipped my tea. The view of Lake Superior was lovely, and it usually calmed me. Not today.

Today...I was worried.

No.

'Worried' didn't encompass the way I felt. I was *petrified*.

Two months before that damn video arrived at our facility, I'd received an email. The subject line had read *Contagious*. It was sent from a now obsolete account. I opened the saved document and re-read the message.

Dear Spider Scientists:

This is not a joke. A new species of tarantula in the Inca jungle is doing all sorts of crazy ~~shit~~ stuff, and you really need to investigate. They're mutating and creating chaos. Thanks for your time. Again, not joking!

-A concerned nature lover

It was laughingly stupid, and neither Francisco nor I had taken it seriously...for good reason. But just eight weeks later, proof had come by way of video file. I'd had my tech team study the footage from beginning to end. It was legitimate. Based on the images, they were able to approximate the area where it was filmed—a small riverside tribal community in Peru.

I'd been breathless with horror as I watched it. When I'd shown it to Francisco, he begged me to send someone else, but he was the only one I trusted to handle such a delicate situation. He'd gone begrudgingly, and now he was dead.

I'd killed him, and I had to live with that knowledge.

Wanting—no, *needing*—to understand what went down in the hospital yesterday, I again opened the video file and, pulse pounding, pushed play.

A shaky image of grass that shifts rapidly toward a rocky outcropping near a stream or river. Lying dead on a smooth stone is a green anaconda. The camera zooms in and focuses on the hairy legs protruding from each side of its muscular body—seven on one side, four on the other. The legs have purplish hair on their femurs. There is no verbal explanation, just the grisly, outrageous footage.

::*Black and white static::*

A piranha thrashing on a fishing hook, its entire body covered in coarse purple hairs. Several shoot from its back as it tries to get free. A fish... shooting urticating hairs.

::*Several seconds of black screen::*

. . .

A new image appears. At the base of some tall bamboo grass, a black spider monkey with a spear wedged between its shoulders, dies sinking its spideresque fangs into a large, brown marsh rat. Black monkey spiders are herbivores.

::More static::

Another image of a large, sturdy tree branch, surrounded by lush greenery. The camera zooms out. Where the branch meets the tree trunk lies a jaguar with an arrow penetrating its side. It's obviously dead. The camera zooms in on the giant feline's face. A blackened tongue lolls from the side of its mouth, and its signature black markings are lost within a plethora of black, soulless spider eyes. A pair of pedipalps grow from its stout neck. Webbing cascades down the side of the tree from the spinnerets beneath the cat's tail.

The viewpoint immediately switches to night vision, and shows hundreds, maybe thousands, of egg sacs inside the body of a rotting llama. The video cuts off as an egg sac bursts open...

::The screen goes black for over a minute, and then...::

A small male child, approximately seven or eight years old, runs through a village near a river. The homes are made from bamboo and straw. A meal is being prepared over a large fire pit in the center of the village. A collared peccary is slowly turning on a spit over the flames. The sun is low in the sky. Singing voices can be heard in the background. They're loud and jovial. Celebratory.

The boy is nude. His body is covered in red liquid. It runs down his torso and legs, dripping onto the sandy ground. A large smile stretches across his face, the skin pulled so tautly, the corners of his mouth have split. He runs toward a heavily pierced, elderly woman and vomits blood into her face, then moves quickly to a tattooed teenage boy and does the same to him.

Then...nothing. He disappears.

The camera jerks back and forth, trying to find the child. It focuses on a young woman breastfeeding an infant. The boy sneaks up behind her and grabs the baby roughly by its neck, pulling it from its mother's grasp. He encircles its ankles with his other hand, holding it like a drumstick, and bites deep into the baby's belly. Ropey intestines hang from his mouth as the mother screams and falls to the ground in a dead faint.

The boy tosses the tiny corpse aside. It lands in the fire pit. Sizzling sounds are heard, along with the rise and fall of a voice in prayer. He projectile vomits on a teenage girl, who appears to be in the early stages of pregnancy. Her partner tries to punch him, but the boy is too fast.

He runs to the river's edge and stops. Seems to convulse in pain. A neon purple spider leg pushes through the back of his neck. Another from his armpit.

A full minute passes as he kneels on the ground.

His eyes look directly at the camera. The cameraman backs away, his ragged breathing loud, and he yells out as the boy sprints toward him...then leaps. His gore-coated skin gets closer and closer to the camera, until there is nothing more than a close-up of his taut abdomen.

Screams are heard, followed by exaggerated grunts and one long groan, as the camera falls to the ground. A dusky blue, late afternoon sky is seen briefly, followed by an emerald-green patch of grass. The screen jostles as the camera hits the ground, then focuses on a man's face, mouth open, missing tongue. His eyes stare blindly into the distance. The boy sits astride his back, eating the tongue, and leering at the camera.

Lines cross the screen, and the image becomes grainy, pixelated. It fades to black, but the audio still functions. Quick, light steps running, the sound growing fainter as they get farther from the camera. Distant sounds of sobbing and panicked chatter are heard.

Minutes pass.

Branches crunching beneath heavy tread.

A man with a heavy accent, "Oh, no. Oh, no! It can't be! The boy was bitten weeks ago!" A loud wail. "We thought he was immune!"

AFTERWORD

Yes, I wrote a killer tarantula novella.

Yes, I do find myself rather loathsome right now.

You see...tarantulas get a bad rap.

Sure, they're big and hairy, have large fangs, and liquify their meals before slurping them up...but they also have precious, cheruby faces (seriously, look at a close-up photo of a tarantula face), like to decorate their homes (which is never the decor *you'd* choose), and enjoy the occasional game of 'Imma throw a ping pong ball into the water dish, Mom.'

Their tiny paws are the absolute cutest, and they even provide comedy relief when they rub their many legs against their abdomens to groom—looks like they're scratching their asses. But the most endearing tarantula behavior I've witnessed is their post-meal celebration. They turn in circles, wiggling their booties back and forth. *Full belly...happy dance time!*

My point? While tarantulas are merciless killers of insects and various types of worms—and really, let's be real, the world needs fewer crickets and hornworms—they have adorable personalities. Most folks never see this, because they can't get past a creature with eight legs and hand-sized bodies. In reality, they're just as much fun as a dog or cat yet require far less maintenance.

I know, because I've raised some myself. I've loved tarantulas most of my life, having purchased my first, a male Chilean Rose named Drac, when I was in high school. Back then, not much was known about keeping tarantulas or the proper husbandry, but I did the best I could, and the two of us did just fine. I still remember the first time he molted. I had no idea they flipped upside down. I thought he'd died! The next day, there he sat snuggling his body double (the molted skin).

Given all the tarantula love, you're probably wondering why Jeff bought me a ball python in April 2024. The answer is simple. I'm a caregiver. I've spent a big portion of my life caring for the people I love...my partners, my kids, my pets, my patients. It's what I know. When I moved to Duluth, I desperately needed a pet to care for, something I could call my own. Jeff had Chaos the Cat, but my adult children, along with my four doggies, were still in West Virginia.

A total sweetheart, Jeff's first offer was to buy my much longed-for tarantula. Unlike pythons, direct heat sources aren't great for our eight-legged friends. We live in Duluth, Minnesota, a beautiful city on Lake Superior I've grown to love, *but*...we're near the Canadian border, and nine months out of the year, the weather ranges from cold to 'I think my nose froze off.' Keeping a tarantula's terrarium the appropriate temperature and humidity would be impossible. So, we found a local breeder, chose our girl, and are now the proud parents of a ball python named Indie Hellspawn McFangy Serenity Strand.

Jeff has promised me four tarantulas in the future...and he's scared of spiders! Which means it's mandatory I get a photo of them crawling all over him. ::ahem::

In conclusion...I'm pro-tarantula, though *Red Inside* may lead you to believe otherwise. After reading this, I bet you'll never again kill any spiders in your house, right? You'll gently pick them up, set them outside, and let them go about their spidery lives, won't you? You'll marvel at their beautiful webs and appreciate all they do to decrease the mosquito population. And then you'll say to yourself, "Bridgett was right! They're not so bad. Maybe I should get a tarantula too!"

I get to name it if you do.

ACKNOWLEDGMENTS

To Parker Nelson - You're a constant source of inspiration for me. I love being your mom, and I'm so incredibly proud of you. Goofy Goobers forever!

To Autumn Nelson - I adore every little thing about you. I hope one day soon you realize just how smart, funny, kind, and beautiful you truly are. Congratulations on the new job! Yay, Harry Styles!

To Christine Morgan - Thanks for always having my back. You're my editor, my harshest critic, and most importantly, one of my best friends.

To Rena Mason - You make *everything* better. Love you, soul sis.

To Richard Dansky - You're the best hugger, my favorite cheese connoisseur, and one of my all-time favorite people in the *entire* world! Woah!

To Ryan Harding, Jay Bower, Eric Butler, and Megan Stockton - Thank you so very much for spending your valuable time reading, blurbing, and promoting my novella...and for making conventions so much fun!

To Jeff Strand - What do I say to the guy who has been there for every up and down of my four-year writing career? You have encouraged me, inspired me, cheered me on, listened to my incessant rambling as I talked out my stories, helped me figure out the self-publishing world, and you've happily read every single word I've ever written. I'm pretty sure you get more excited about my successes than your own! You are, without a doubt, the best friend and partner I could have ever asked for. I love you. Thanks for being my happy.

And finally, to everyone who has loved me, stood by me, and supported me without judgment, I'm forever grateful.

ABOUT THE AUTHOR

Once an operating room registered nurse, Bridgett Nelson so enjoyed playing with human organs, she decided to turn her macabre interest into a horror writing career. She loves bubble baths (because nothing says spooky writer like orange-scented bubbles), hates not knowing what's swimming in the water with her, lives for Halloween season (but loathes chainsaw-wielding dudes in haunted houses), adores her West Virginia University Mountaineers, is very pro-Oxford comma, and thinks bananas are absolutely disgusting.

Her first collection, ***A Bouquet of Viscera***, is a two-time Splatterpunk Award winner, recognized both for the collection itself and its standout story, "Jinx." ***Deadgirl***, the novelization of the cult classic film is now available from Encyclopocalypse Publications and includes forewords from the film's actors, Noah Segan and Shiloh Fernandez, a Q&A from screenwriter, Trent Haaga, and a fan fiction piece from Bram Stoker Award-winning horror author, Jeff Strand. Also available is her latest collection, **Embracing the Profane**, which includes fifteen extreme stories that play on Bridgett's dark humor and twisted brain. She's also authored **Poisoned Pink**, **What the Fuck Was That?**, **Sweet, Sour, & Spicy**, and **Red Inside**, a finalist in the 2025 Books of Horror Indie Brawl.

Her work has appeared in multiple anthologies, including the iconic *Deathrealm Spirits*, Crystal Lake's *Hotel Macabre*, Edward Lee's *Erotic Horror for Horny Housewives*, *The Rack*, *GhabaGhoul*, *To Hell and Back*, *Evil Little Fucks*, *Y'all Ain't Right*, *Splatterpunk's Basement of Horror*, *Dark Disasters*, *October Screams*, *American Cannibal*, *A Woman Unbecoming*, and the legendary *Splatterpunk Zine*.

Bridgett is working on her first original novel, a sequel novel to her most popular short story, and a collaborative novel with a very funny writer.

Bridgett is mom to Parker and Autumn, three pugs, a Saint Bernard, and a ball python. She is a 2022 Michael Knost WINGS award nominee, won second place in the '22 Gross-Out contest at KillerCon in Austin, Texas, and third place in the '23 Gross-Out contest.

She's a freelance editor. Audiobook proofer. Bookworm. Dog lover. Tarantula whisperer. Bra avoider. ENJF. Amaretto Sour obsessor.

Bridgett currently lives in Duluth, Minnesota, with horror author, Jeff Strand, and their pretty ball python daughter, Indie Hellspawn McFangy Serenity Strand.

Also By Bridgett Nelson...

DEADGIRL

Once deemed too controversial to release, *Deadgirl* stunned festival audiences, outraged religious groups, and became an instant cult sensation. A film that seared itself into the minds of the depraved and the discerning alike, it remains one of the most transgressive and boundary-pushing nightmares of its era.

When two high school misfits—bound by boredom and adolescent hunger— ditch class to slip beyond the rusted doors of an abandoned hospital, they stumble upon a gruesome secret that will shatter their innocence and test the limits of their sanity: a woman, stripped bare and chained to a table.

She's abandoned. She's beautiful. She's dead ...or is she?

Celebrated author Bridgett Nelson breathes new life into Trent Haaga's infamous, unholy fever dream—a harrowing exploration of intimacy, morality, and the horrors of growing up. *Deadgirl* is a grotesque coming-of-age nightmare that peels back the skin of innocence to expose the raw, throbbing horror beneath.

You can look away. You can tell yourself it's only a story. You may deny what it reveals about you.

But Deadgirl will still be there—waiting.

Praise for *Deadgirl*:

"Bridgett Nelson's novelization delves deeper into the world Trent created, and I am thrilled that she took on this project. Her transformation of the film is an exciting new chapter for our *Deadgirl*. Her writing fills out the world we all dared to build those years ago—the provocative, unflinching themes, conflicts, and haunting questions that lingered long after the original story ended. She has masterfully expanded the narrative, revealing aspects of the story that are only hinted at in the movie. Her adaptation delves into the psychological and moral complexities that the film could only touch upon, offering a richer, more nuanced exploration of the characters and their world. I believe this novel will resonate more powerfully today as society grapples with increasingly polarized debates about ethics, consent, and the essence of human nature." – **Shiloh Fernandez, 'Rickie'**

"Bridgett's work tracks a slippery slope from disenfranchised, vulnerable people to the unimaginable horrors they're put through. What Bridgett has done, through Ivy's story, is humanize a character whose humanity was stolen. In doing so, she added a new layer of horror, but also one of sympathy. This novelization, and its backstory, are studies in the cycles of trauma. We've come far in terms of what we expect from our boys, and how we teach our children to treat one another. Not far enough, obviously, but as we evolve, this film and novelization will hopefully serve more as a fable than a cautionary tale." – **Noah Segan, 'JT**

"Some books push boundaries. Others obliterate them. *Deadgirl* is the latter." – **Honey Dy, Goodreads Review**

"A brutal masterpiece that will break and haunt you. Some books whisper warnings. *Deadgirl* kicks the damn door in. I went into this without seeing the film, and honestly? I'm glad. Bridgett Nelson doesn't just adapt a cult classic—she resurrects it, injects it with pain, purpose, and poetry, and gives the silenced girl at its center a soul. Ivy Reyes isn't just "the Deadgirl" anymore. She's real. She's angry. And she's unforgettable." – **Robin Ginther-Vinneri, Goodreads Review**

"Bridgett has taken this *Deadgirl*, worked her magical CPR, and resuscitated new life into a once thought, long-lost corpse! Well and truly worth your time, people." – **Simon Dower, Goodreads Review**

EMBRACING THE PROFANE

She may be soft-hearted and bubbly, but **Splatterpunk Award-winner Bridgett Nelson** knows how to *horrify*.

She knows how to *disturb*.

And she sure as hell knows how to *make you squirm*.

She proved it with *A Bouquet of Viscera*. And again with *Poisoned Pink*. Now she's taking it to the next grisly level with *Embracing the Profane*, fifteen stories that will grab you by the throat...and rip it right out, one piece of viscera at a time.

Want deviant sex? She's got you covered. "Cherrified" is every man's worst nightmare. Up for a little bestiality? "Can't Be Tamed" is the one for you! No-holds-barred depravity? Check out "Hot for Cold."

She'll break your heart with "Dying River." And you'll wonder what the ever-loving fuck is wrong with her once you've read "Shits N' Giggles."

Like the 1980s AIDS epidemic, "Let's Hear It for the Boy" brings confrontation and controversy. Want characters you'll love to hate? The cruel bullies in "Three, Two, One..." are sure to scratch that itch.

Go on.

Join her.

Embrace the profane.

What's the worst that can happen?

Praise for *Embracing the Profane*:

"Bridgett Nelson has tapped into same severed vein as Monica J. O'Rourke, Charlee Jacob, and C.V. Hunt, proving once again that the female of the species can be just as depraved and unholy as the males. *Embracing the Profane* is a grotesque menagerie of horrors, crafted with the cruelest of intentions, with splatters of dark comedy to tickle the blackest of souls. If you want unrelenting, revolting, extreme horror, Bridgett Nelson is here to smack you in the face with it." – **Kristopher Triana, author of *Full Brutal***

"This collection dives into themes of depravity and inhumanity, presenting stories that are as visceral as they are emotionally charged. And so relatable it's concerning, at times. Nelson's writing refuses to shy away from the uncomfortable, instead confronting readers head-on with stark depictions of humanity's shadowed facets. Each story unfolds with a raw intensity that makes it difficult to put the book down at any point. And the depth Nelson skillfully achieves in such a short work ensures that the terror experienced is vivid and immersive, often visceral in its descriptions. The world-building and imagery gives you a front-row-seat to the insanity. Which only heightens the sense of dread and discomfort. Bridgett Nelson crafts stories that are horrifying yet thought-provoking, pushing readers to confront uncomfortable and profane truths about human nature. For those willing to engage with its challenging content, this book offers a compelling and unforgettable reading experience." – **Amanda Rusza, author of *I Hope You Have Nightmares About Me***

POISONED PINK

From **Bridgett Nelson**, the two-time Splatterpunk Award-winning author of *A BOUQUET OF VISCERA*, **POISONED PINK** combines the acclaimed, bestselling collections *WHAT THE FUCK WAS THAT?* and *SWEET, SOUR, & SPICY* into one venomous package!

A famous author holds a contest to have characters named after his biggest fans – but after the book is published, the fans begin to die exactly as their characters did. A childhood friendship turns terrifyingly dark, and stalking is taken to a demented new level. A deranged serial killer has a special affinity for a deadly – and heinous – weapon. Two college heartthrobs are thrilled by the completely unexpected sex games their girlfriends want to play...until things go much too far.

Also included is the bonus story, "Ambush," in which we learn that the creatures of the ocean are even more frightening and dangerous than we thought.

Do you dare to enter Bridgett Nelson's lair? If so, prepare to get caught in her nightmarish web...

POISONED PINK. This lady is deadly.

PRAISE FOR *POISONED PINK*:

"Who wants a kick in the balls? If you just raised your hand and said, "I do! I do!" I've got just the author for you. Once in a blue moon, a horror writer hits the scene and shakes everything up. In Extreme Horror, that writer would be Bridgett Nelson. She writes the most horrifying, outrageous, offensive, down-and-dirtiest horror I've ever seen. Aberrant sex, belly-emptying violence, psycho-killers with boners, zoophilia, and even a dildo shaped makes one wonder what REALLY makes the human species tick. This is BALL-BUSTING horror fiction, folks (even if you don't HAVE balls), and it will grab you by the ears, push your face into one heaping, steaming pile of horror after another, and force you to eat. Don't believe me? Give Bridgett Nelson a try, but don't forget your vomit bag... "– **Edward Lee, author of *The Bighead* and *Header*.**

"Bridgett Nelson's work is about as f**ked up as it gets. If you can handle it, you're in for a wonderfully deranged and gruesome treat. If you can't handle it, I understand." - **Jeff Strand, Bram Stoker Award-winning author of *Twentieth Anniversary Screening***

"Giggly kicked my ass. Outstanding job! I need therapy now." - **Edward Lee, author of *The Bighead* and *Header***

A Bouquet of Viscera

2023 Splatterpunk Award Winner for Best Collection and Best Short Story ("Jinx")!

An overzealous vigilante, who sees her victims' auras, finds herself in a very uncomfortable situation. A young woman, injected with a microchip in a futuristic America, develops unusual and grisly cravings. Four high school graduates end up on the menu of a giant, mutant sea creature. Diary entries share shocking and disturbing confessions…but who is the author?

Bridgett Nelson, a fresh new talent in the world of horror, makes her debut with this short fiction collection containing these stories and more! These gory tales of revenge and retribution are sure to terrify and delight readers in equal measure.

Before opening the pages of **A BOUQUET OF VISCERA**, be sure to take a deep, calming breath. Because these nightmare scenarios, and many others, are lurking under the covers and waiting just for you.

Foreword by Ronald Kelly.

Praise for *A Bouquet of Viscera*:

"From genuinely disturbing body horror, to savage sea creatures, to grisly satire and much more, this absolutely stellar collection has something for any horror fan who's ready to be kicked in the gut. It's dark stuff, sometimes very dark, so don't come crying to me if you can't handle it!" **– Jeff Strand, author of *Clowns Vs. Spiders***

"Gnarly and excellent, the stories in A BOUQUET OF VISCERA will grab you by the throat and not let you go." **- Richard Dansky, author of *Nightmare Logic & Ghost of a Marriage***

"A solid collection with tales of revenge, body horror, psychosis, conspiracies, ghosts, and even a creature feature. I admire the eclectic, Books of Blood-esque nature of the collection, but the

pervading theme is vengeance; specifically, bad guys getting their comeuppance." **– Nick Roberts, award-winning and best-selling author of *The Exorcist's House* and *Mean-Spirited***

"Bridgett Nelson's debut fiction collection, *A Bouquet of Viscera*, presents a set of horror tales that range from the darkly fanciful to the most deeply, personally disturbing. There's not a single tale that doesn't hit most or all the right notes. Many of the stories draw upon her real-life experience in the medical field to build a believable — and usually unsettling — backdrop." **– Stephen Mark Rainey, author of *The House at Black Tooth Pond* and *The Gods of Moab***

"Macabre and intense, *A Bouquet of Viscera* is a fantastic collection of extreme horror. With plenty of blood, gore, and suspenseful plot twists, each story will hook you and hold you hostage. From deadly fungus to underwater monsters and deranged psychopaths, this book has something for everyone." **– Kayla Frederick, best-selling author of *Memento Mori: 13 Tales of Terror* and *The Residency***

"*A Bouquet of Viscera* is for horror fans who like their fiction with an edge and who aren't afraid to get cut." **– Lionel Ray Green, *Fresh Blood***

www.ingramcontent.com/pod-product-compliance
Lightning Source LLC
Chambersburg PA
CBHW030314160726
47992CB00005B/2004